COLD WORLD

DENNIS VOGEN

This book is dedicated to everyone
who lives life for life itself.

This is a work of fiction.

Names, characters, places, and incidents either are the
product of the author's imagination or are used fictitiously.
Any resemblance to actual persons, living or dead, events, or
locals is entirely coincidental.

First eBook edition June 2022

First paperback & hardcover edition June 2022

Cover photography by Steven Starks, Jr.

Cover design by Steven Starks, Jr. and Dennis Vogen

Book design by Dennis Vogen

Published by Dennis Vogen, Sleeping Kitty Productions

www.dennisvogen.com

Special Thanks to my Co-Publishers

Chris Anderson, Julia Androff, Baby Skullcrusher (Mia Romani), Brenda Brisley & Family, D.P. Brown, Kyle Casello, Kristi Coughlin, Melissa Cindric, Katie Downs, Dragonsteel Entertainment, Brent Dubé, Bekah Fitz, Questor German, Rodney & Missy Guenther, Lauren Hall, Krista Hanner, Ben Johnson, Jeffrey Jones, Mariah Kaercher, Amy Kielmeyer, Kody Kile & the Kile Family, Ryan Knott, George M. Landais, Chris McColley, Andy Meissner, Poly Mendes, Kyle & Nora of Noggin Comics, Jason Eddie Nowak, Danielle Nutt, Alyx Paschke, Nicole Scissons, Amanda Schaner-Martinez, Steven Starks Jr, Debra Stevenson Silvernale, The Stocker Family, David Swisher, Shaun Thibodeau, Jason Dean Thomas, Richard Titus, Amy Vogen, Blair Warnemunde, Neal Wertanen, Roger Whiting, James Wobschall

This book doesn't exist without you.

Thank You

My family

My friends

My supporters

I don't exist without you.

Table of Contents

1

There is a moment, in the cold, as you lose the feeling in your fingers and toes, when you will never have felt more alive. This sensation also serves as a reminder that you will soon be dead.

Calef's extremities were tingling as he approached Oscar's house, his boots crunching in the ever-present snow. On his left side, he carried a painting wrapped in paper; on his right bounced his beloved dog, a Golden Saint named Joan. Joan weighed over two hundred pounds, a healthy girl; her underside was waves of white, the rest of her covered in thick brushstrokes of reddish-brown fur. Two black diamonds traced her bright, hazel eyes. Joan was inarguably Calef's best friend. Calef considered himself a wanderer, a stray atom; Joan was his inescapable proton.

Calef's second-best friend, Rebecca, was waiting in Oscar's yard, her face subtly shifting, from following her ascending breath to melting with joy upon seeing Joan's black snout.

"Joanie!" Rebecca shouted, her voice echoing down the dark, empty street, lit only by streetlamp and snowflakes. She ran down to greet them, Joan jumping to meet Rebecca, landing on top of her and slamming her backwards into a pile of powder. Calef stopped, shook his head, and offered Rebecca a hand.

"She loves me more than you," Rebecca sang.

"You keep telling yourself that," Calef said and then laughed.

The three of them walked up to Oscar's doors, a glass one separating them from a wooden one. Joan admired the beauty of her humans in the reflection: Calef, dark-skinned, a neatly trimmed black beard framing his face and lips; he had equally black hair on his head, also neat, but nearing the point of needing a scissors. He was wearing an unzipped neon green jacket with a navy hooded sweatshirt underneath. Then Joan looked at Rebecca, her amber hair tucked under a teal winter hat, hands covered in red mittens tucked in her matching teal coat. Her pale skin had patches of blush where warmth exploded in flashes, mostly in her cheeks. Then Joan looked at herself, and remembered what a good girl she was. She smiled. Oscar's door opened.

"Happy birthday, Oscar!" Calef and Rebecca said in unison as Joan barked to be included. They stomped the outdoors off their boots before taking them off and putting them in a pile next to the door.

Oscar was turning eighty-five-years-old; he was old enough to remember when the Earth had four seasons.

"What do you want to do tonight, old man?" Calef asked as he leaned his painting against the yellow living room wall.

"They're doin' a story on TV about the eightieth anniversary of the asteroid at seven . . ."

Oscar said. He smiled while avoiding eye contact, trailing off hopefully.

"I thought you were there, old man," Calef teased him.

"I was," Oscar said, becoming serious.

"Of course we can watch TV for a little while," Rebecca said, elbowing Calef in the ribs. "But you promised we'd have dinner and play some cards, too, and that's why we're here."

"Okay, then," Oscar relented. "I just want to watch for a few minutes and then I'll beat your asses at cards. TV, on. Oven, pre-heat."

At his voice commands, the television and oven woke up. An infomercial for genetic appearance modification ended and an advertisement for a new model of lasergun followed; then a woman with short purple hair and big teeth, possibly a product of the aforementioned genetic appearance modification, appeared on the screen.

"Good evening," she started. "Thank you for joining us today, June 2nd, 2222."

An old video showed a massive explosion. Oscar's eyes filled with tears.

"As our viewers know," she continued, "it has been eighty years today since Australia was impacted by a large asteroid known as Velos. That day changed our existence as we knew it. Through a chain reaction of subsequent events, Earth was plunged into a permanent winter.

"By this time, most of humanity had already left Earth for the other places we had colonized, largely thanks to the Knights of Christianity and their billionaire prophet, Jonah Mesh; we had developed homes on several moons, Mars, and an uninhabited, Earth-like planet previously known as Proxima b, which we now know as Flora.

"We realized the potential of Flora as a livable habitat through the use of laser-propelled lightsails that had been sent to Alpha Centauri decades prior. It wasn't until we were able to develop and utilize wormhole technology that even traveling there could be a possibility. Large ships and smaller shuttles, thanks to the continued generosity of groups like the

Knights, now travel there and back on a regular basis.

"By the time our scientists were able to predict the approach of Velos, the Earth had a population of less than a billion people. Even though we were able to prepare ourselves, and even accurately map several possible locations of the impact, the Earth lost a quarter of that population in the first year, some in the initial collision, and some in the aftermath.

"But humanity did not only survive; we adapted, and then we thrived.

"We were able to use technology in every facet of our lives, from the clean nuclear- and wind-power we utilize, to the artificial greenhouses, to the hover capabilities of our vehicles, to the popular Viking DNA mod, which gives Earthers born after the impact a set of biological advantages for living in the cold.

"An everlong cold that has shown no sign of ending, year after year."

The reporter couldn't hide a sense of hopelessness in her face at these words.

"Can we turn this off now?" Calef asked.

"Sure," Oscar answered, snapped out of a trance triggered by memories. Joan crawled over to him and placed her soft head under his hand, which resumed a naturally occurring petting pattern. They walked together into the kitchen. Oscar appreciated her warmth. He knew that she kept Calef's cold, yin nature in balance.

"Coffee, brew," Oscar grumbled, and his machine started grinding specialty beans grown on Flora that a neighbor had gifted him for his special day.

"I'll deal," Rebecca offered.

"You'll cheat," Oscar said. "Calef deals."

They sat on either side of an old table made with thick, knotted wood, on long, sturdy benches with low backs. Oscar sat down next to Calef, and Joan sat on the bench next to Rebecca. Oscar looked wary.

"She'll be good," Rebecca said, referring to the dog on the bench.

"I'm not worried about the dog," Oscar pointed at Rebecca.

Rebecca was brilliant, an actual scientist, the head of a general research department at the University of Minnesota. But she was also mischievous, impatient, and fond of finding loopholes which, in a game, most other people would define as cheating.

The U was on the east side of Minneapolis, but Oscar, Calef and Rebecca all lived in a neighborhood on the west.

"If she gets out of hand, I'll tie her up to a tree outside," Calef promised Oscar of Rebecca. "It's a nice night. I don't think she'll freeze."

Oscar laughed. He rubbed his face, the wrinkles on his dark skin stretching up and down, giving several quick glimpses to what he may have looked like when his skin clung tighter to his body.

He had short silver hair, a striking contrast to the shadows in the creeks of his face.

"Where's the boy with the blue hair?" Oscar asked.

"I'm surprised you're wondering where Alva is," Calef remarked, sharing a smile with Rebecca.

"Why's that?" Oscar asked.

"Because he always seems to annoy the shit out of you," Rebecca said.

"He does," Oscar agreed. "But he's a good kid."

"Do you think he *like* likes me, though?" a voice from beyond the kitchen asked. Alva, the blue-haired boy, appeared as though summoned from a lamp.

"Goddamn it," Oscar swore, having immediate regret for speaking of the devil. Alva kissed the old man on the cheek, then narrowly avoided an open-handed slap across his own. Everyone laughed. Joan gave Alva kisses on the mouth, which he gladly received.

Alva's grandparents had emigrated to the United States from Korea after the asteroid hit, starting a restaurant business that had evolved, or entropized, into the college bar that Alva now ran. His skin was golden, his smile was radiant, his wit was sharp as a skate.

"It smells good in here," Alva noted while gently wrapping his hand behind Rebecca's shoulder. She was the only person Alva was gentle with. She didn't know what that meant and it made her furious.

"It did smell good until your stanky ass slid its way across my floor," Oscar said.

"I think my stanky ass improved the quality of the stank in here considerably," Alva countered.

The two continued to banter until they all heard a growing hum coming from outside the house. It evolved from a dull purr to a dense roar as it grew closer to them, seemingly from above, the walls around them vibrating. Joan's ears slid back.

They put their gear on and opened the front door, which was doused in a bright light. They stepped towards it.

"Shit," Calef said.

"What is it?" Rebecca asked.

In front of them was a large spacecraft known as a Sea Eagle, easily capable of transporting hundreds of people. In a genius affront to aerodynamic design, it resembled a massive, metallic honeycomb. It was hovering a few dozen meters over the ground, loud, demanding of attention. On the side of the ship was the symbol of the Knights of Christianity. Under the craft, a door opened and a small elevator carrying a handful of people descended. When they reached the ground, they started to approach Oscar's house.

"You know these people, Calef?" Alva asked.

"I should hope so," the man leading the party said. His complexion was matched by his long, black robe, with a thick golden line descending down each shoulder. He smiled with glorious purpose.

"My name is Abe. I am Calef's father."

2

"So . . . are you going to invite me in?"

Abe stood in the snow with three other Knights.

"I would, dad," Calef said. "But this isn't my house."

"This *is* mine," Oscar said, "and I am freezing my wrinkly ass off, so let's all get inside where it's warm."

His friends and the Knights followed Oscar into the house.

. . .

Calef, Joan, Rebecca and Alva took a seat on a bench on one side of the table; the four Knights sat down on the other. Oscar grabbed some assorted mugs from a cabinet and started pouring coffee into them.

"You could have called, pops," Calef said.

"Would you have answered?" Abe asked. Calef averted his eyes and sighed. "I do apologize for crashing your party." Abe pointed to a small cake on the kitchen counter, with two candles on top in the shape of the numbers eight and five.

"Nah, this is exciting," Oscar said and smiled, sipping his coffee. "A birthday bash and a family reunion all in the same day."

"You guys are all hard over God, right?" Alva asked, grabbing some potato chips from a bag on the table and shoving them in his mouth. Rebecca elbowed him in the side, which most people would receive as a signal to stop, but Alva took as solid encouragement.

Abe ignored the question about being sexually aroused by his lord and savior.

"These are my fellow Knights," he said, gesturing down the line from him. "This is Joe, Maya, and Minister Will Mather."

Joe looked like any white soldier (or cop) Calef had ever seen; buzz-cut, square-jaw, shadows under his nose and eyes.

Calef made the mistake of staring at Maya for too long when they were outside, studying her caramel skin and thickly braided hair. Formally introduced, he smiled, then bobbed his head with his lips too tight, and then smiled again, too big, too open. Maya radiated without effort, bringing the sunshine from Flora with her.

The first thing he wanted to tell her was how beautiful she was, but she also seemed like a woman who did not care about subjective opinions on external beauty, which he intimately understood was part of her appeal.

Calef immediately distrusted Minister Will Mather and his slick hair, which looked possibly glued to his scalp. Will sat there stiff, but likely believed himself to be poised; his voice was both reedy and robotic, and Calef sensed there was dark depth to him that he didn't want to sink to find.

"Thank you for that introduction, Abe," Will said. "Usually, I would never let another person speak for me when meeting someone new, but these are special circumstances, as you are family. As sole minister, I am the leader of this expedition of Knights."

At this, Rebecca perked up.

"So what brings you back to our little part of the galaxy?" she asked. Will looked annoyed at her participation.

"It's complicated, so I'll try to make this as simple as I can," Will said.

"Thank you," Alva said, "and please dooo speeeak slooow so even a dum-dum like me can follow along." Will took a deep breath.

"Our visit is two-fold. The first reason is a simple survey. Our drones have determined that the Velos asteroid site in Australia is safe for human beings to visit now."

"People have been living down there for years," Rebecca added.

"Safe for us, I mean," Will said. "We're going to visit the site ourselves, get samples, take photos, do a complete survey on behalf of the Knights and the planet of Flora, for both research and posterity."

"I don't understand what I have to do with that," Calef said.

"Nothing," Will said. "You have nothing to do with that part. If you'll let me finish."

Calef looked to Joan with eyes that asked, "Is he serious?"

Joan grumbled.

"The second part is the prophecy we discovered," Abe said, with all the conviction of a Knight.

"Jonah Mesh, the founder of the Knights, was a prolific prophet," Will went on, his eyes wide at Abe for the further interruption. "He wrote and spoke so many words that we're still going through them now, years and years after his death. Recently, we discovered both a prediction and a solution."

"For what?" Calef asked.

"Long before it happened," Will said, placing his palms out in front of himself, "Jonah prophesized that an asteroid would strike Earth, and he predicted the cold that would fall upon this world."

"Why didn't he tell no one?" Oscar asked, long-held anger in his voice.

"He did," Abe said. "Nobody believed him."

"But you said there's a solution," Calef said, with the hesitancy you use towards a person you know is selling you on a pyramid scheme.

"Jonah shared that buried under the Great Lakes of America, there is a sleeping phoenix," Will said. "And those who wake the great phoenix will bring warmth back to this world."

Calef and his friends sat silently on the other side of the table.

And then spontaneously burst into the kind the laughter you save for an emergency.

"Okay, dad," Calef said, "You and your friends have had your fun. It was great seeing you after all this time, but we do have a card game to get back to, so we wish you a good night and a good life."

"Son," Abe said, "on your mother's name, I have never been more serious about anything."

"Everyone but my father needs to get out," Calef said.

The air froze between the men. Carefully, the entire room stood up and left the kitchen.

"How fucking dare you?" Calef asked.

"I'm sorry to bring up your mother's memory – " Abe started.

"Are you?" Calef asked. "You seemed pretty damn ready to play that card out your sleeve."

"I admit, I knew it was going to be hard to convince you," Abe said.

"You knew right," Calef confirmed. "Why me? Why do you need me? Why are you here?"

"Because of your . . . history, I know that you are the most qualified person to guide us across the Great Lakes." Abe's hand was face up on the table now.

"Y'all are scared of the Neo Atheists, then," Calef said.

"Of course we are," Abe confessed. "We hear the stories, we follow your news."

"It's not all true," Calef said.

"But if even half of it is . . ." Abe said, trailing off, thinking of the horrors he had heard and seen of the Neo Atheists. He tried to laugh it off. "You thought you were mad at me for bringing up your mom? I . . . I brought your sisters with me, too."

"Are you fucking crazy, dad?" Caleb asked. "You brought my sister and my brother with you?"

"Yes, Calef," Abe said, correcting himself. "That is what I meant to say. Your sister and your brother are here on the Sea Eagle, too."

"Goddamn it," Caleb said.

"Watch your mouth," Abe snapped.

"Read the room," Calef snapped back. He paced around the kitchen. "You're not really giving me a choice here. It's not safe. I'm not going to let anything happen to you."

"So you'll come?" Abe asked. Calef collapsed onto the bench, arms draped over the back, defeated.

"Wait."

Rebecca and Joan walked back into the kitchen; they had been listening from behind a wall. Joan took her place next to Calef, who scratched her behind the ears. She licked his face, reminding him that she was prepared to protect her friend, wherever he needed to be.

"We'll go, but we also want to see the site in Australia," Rebecca added.

"Deal," Abe said.

"Hold on a minute," another voice came barging back into the room, this one belonging to Will. "This was not the agreement, Abe."

"We never had an agreement," Calef said. "But we do now. Me, Joan, and Rebecca will do this for you but Rebecca, the scientist, gets to decide the terms."

"Oh, fuck you," Alva's voice climbed and pushed over the others. "I'm going, too." He grabbed another handful of chips and fed them to Joan.

"Will, we need them," Abe said. "We cannot let pride be our downfall here. My son and his friends know this place like nobody on Flora can. This mission is too important."

Will considered it for a moment.

"Fine," Will said, throwing his hands up in the air. Rebecca and Alva cheered, Joan barked, and Calef just shook his head. "We're leaving now. There is food and clothing and supplies on the Sea Eagle. This should not be a long trip."

"You hear that, old man?" Calef shouted to Oscar. "We'll be back before you know it, and we'll finish celebrating your birthday then. Don't die."

Oscar was watching TV, lost in the narrative he lived as a child. Calef's words brought him back to Earth.

"Take the painting with you," Oscar said.

"What?" Calef asked. "But it's your gift."

"Trust me," he said, pulling Calef closer and giving him a kiss on the top of his head.

. . .

Calef, painting in hand, alongside Joan, Rebecca, and Alva, followed the Knights back to the Sea Eagle. As they got on the elevator to take them up, Calef turned around to see Oscar standing in his doorway, behind the glass.

Calef could clearly see that Oscar was giving them the finger.

3

As a son, Calef was frustrated by this new responsibility placed upon his shoulders. As a wanderer, however, he started to find himself excited by the possibilities of letting himself go.

The elevator brought the eight of them up into the ship, lifting them through a dark garage to another level. Once the door underneath them shut and sealed, the sound of another door depressurizing signaled for them to walk forward onto the main deck of the ship, known as the Chest.

It was a massive, mostly white, well-lit room, with open stairways and several levels being utilized by dozens of people; they wore clothing in a variety of colors, but all adorned with gold in some fashion. The Chest was the beating heart of the ship, with walls of screens and touchpads used for everything from navigation to setting the temperature in each cabin and hallway. Small drones floated from station to station, some carrying data, others cups of coffee. Calef and his friends had to pause to look up and take it all in.

"Gather around," Minister Will Mather said to his crew. "This is Calef, Abe's son, and his friends, Rebecca and Alva." Joan whined. "And his dog."

The people who had been hurrying on the floor of the Chest stopped to form a semi-circle around the Minister.

"They know this area and its people better than anyone from Flora could. They will be our guides when we reach the Great Lakes. But first, we will be heading to Toowoomba in Australia to survey the Velos site. We will leave immediately. ETA is a few hours."

The crew resumed their business.

"Let me take you to your cabins," Abe said. Calef and his friends followed behind him, still taken by awe at the sights of the ship. The front of the Chest had massive video screens that acted like a windshield, in which they could see the view outside; each side of the room had multiple levels of doorways that led to hallways. Some of those walkways led to work and recreation rooms, but most of them led to cabins, where the crew of the Sea Eagle could rest. Abe took Calef and his friends into a hall of empty rooms.

"Here's where you all will be staying," Abe said. "There are three open rooms here, unless Joan here wanted her own." Joan licked Abe's hand, fully appreciating his sense of humor.

"I think she'll be fine with me, pops," Calef assured him.

"Will mentioned there would be more clothes and supplies on the ship?" Rebecca reminded him.

"Yes," Abe said. "At the back of the Chest are rooms with everything you need, including food. You can eat in those back rooms with the rest of the crew, or bring food back to your cabin. Though, I believe fellowship is important, so I do hope you try to get to know some of us from Flora."

"Thank you, Abe," Rebecca said, turning to Calef. "I'm going to see what they have. I'll have to call the U, too, and tell them you and I will be out for a few days."

The University of Minnesota had always been a significant piece of their lives. Rebecca and Calef had met there as students and were now part of their faculty; Rebecca was a research scientist whose bounds knew no particular field, and Calef taught in the art department. Oscar, though now retired, had also been on the U staff.

"I'll come with you," Alva said. The bar he ran, Gelid Society, was a few blocks from campus. When Rebecca and Calef met him, he was a snot-nosed bartender who rarely made them pay their tab; since then, he had inherited ownership of the bar from his father.

Rebecca and Alva went back out the way they came, both sharing a look with Calef to make sure he was okay. Calef nodded.

"Could I speak with you, son?" Abe asked.

Calef knew what was coming. There were times in his life when he and his dad had deep conversations, and since his mother died and his family moved from Earth to Flora without him, it had been years since they had one.

When these talks occurred, Calef no longer felt like a participant in a normal conversation; he felt like he was an actor in a play, words exchanged so precise and cutting that his subconscious must have written them beforehand. He could feel, in this moment, a curtain rise. His skin felt hot under the imagined lights. After a few last-minute coughs and crinkles of paper, the first act begun.

Act I

CALEF and ABE enter an empty cabin. In the room, there is a bunk bed, a couch and a chair. CALEF sets his painting in a corner and returns to center stage.

CALEF: What's up, dad?

ABE: I've been worried about you.

CALEF: Recently? Or my entire life?

ABE: There is nothing wrong with wanting to save your child.

CALEF: There is if he doesn't want to be saved.

ABE: Did I ever tell you the story –

CALEF: – if it's from the Bible, then yes, you did. I've heard them all. It's like gossip, pops. Soap opera. Sex and murder and cheating and lies.

ABE sits down in the chair. A beat.

ABE: I'm just trying to help you see the truth.

CALEF: And I'm trying to tell you that your truth doesn't feel true to me.

ABE: When your mother died, I didn't know what to do.

CALEF: Me, neither. Clearly.

ABE: But I knew I wanted to be closer to her.

CALEF: By running away?

ABE: That's not what I did.

CALEF: Earth was her home, dad. You took my siblings and you moved to another planet.

ABE: I needed to be with people who believed in what I believed.

CALEF: And what about the people who believed in you? The human being you? You're a good person, dad.

ABE: I am fallible. I am full of sin.

CALEF: I don't believe in sin.

ABE: You are wrong.

CALEF: That's debatable.

ABE: Not to me.

CALEF: That's the thing. You can never be wrong, because what you believe can never be proven or disproven. There are no facts in your faith, just feelings. But not being wrong doesn't mean you're right about anything, either, and you certainly have no right to contradict the things that we know for sure. That's why we have so many problems.

ABE: We have one problem. I know the problem. Our problem is sin. The solution is salvation. I found that on Flora. I find that in God.

CALEF: Do you know what Oscar does?

ABE: That man you were with when we found you?

CALEF: My friend, yes. He's a world religions scholar.

ABE: And what kind of nonsense has he told you?

CALEF: None. He has told me no nonsense. He's only given me power.

ABE: And what power is that?

CALEF: Look, everyone thinks power is a different thing. Money is power. Knowledge is power. Salvation is power. Power is power.

CALEF sits down on the bed.

CALEF: For me, understanding is power. Understanding is what gives all the other powers power. And I understand.

ABE: What is it that you understand?

CALEF: To survive, we have to use any tool that works. I think people who decide that what they believe is the right thing blind themselves to everything else. Your thing isn't wrong, dad. Your thing is incomplete.

ABE: My God is perfect.

CALEF: Then why does he change?

ABE: You don't know what you're talking about.

CALEF: Don't I? I don't believe in your God and yet I try to understand Him, anyway. How many people try to understand the other people and other things that go against what they believe?

ABE leans back in his chair.

CALEF: I tried to understand you. And my sister and my brother. I tried to understand how you could leave mom's home behind. How you could leave me behind.

ABE: We didn't leave you behind . . .

CALEF: Then what do you call it?

ABE: We followed our hearts. We followed God.

CALEF: So then it was God who abandoned me?

ABE: He cannot make someone follow Him . .

.

CALEF: . . . and yet you can't stop trying.

ABE: I just want us all to be together in Heaven.

CALEF: And you're willing to sacrifice what we have here, now.

Calef felt eyes on him, as his eyes were beginning to burn with tears. He turned to see his friends standing in his cabin's doorway.

"You okay?" Rebecca asked.

"Yeah," Calef said. "We're done here."

Abe took his cue, stood up and began to walk out of the room. When he reached the door, the entire floor shook. Joan barked.

"What the fuck was that?" Alva asked.

They all ran down the hallway back to the Chest. The crew was looking up at the massive video screens, trying to figure out the source of the quake. Another tremor hit, sending several people to their knees.

Suddenly, a few massive drones, the size of a single-passenger airplane, dropped into view. They were firing lasers at the Sea Eagle.

"Air pirates," Joe, the soldier from earlier, said.

"Worse," Calef said. "Those are Neo Atheists."

4

A wave of terror jolted the crew.

"They're calling us," Ada said, pushing a pair of purple glasses up her nose, her bhutlah pepper-colored skin immediately slick with a light coat of sweat. The communications chief was about half the height of the tallest man on the ship and twice as loud.

"Send them –" Will started.

"Do not engage," Calef interrupted. Will's arm shot around, his finger aimed directly at Calef.

"You do not run this ship, boy," Will said back.

"*Boy?!*" Calef repeated. Abe got between his son and the minister.

"Like I was saying, Ada," Will continued, "send them through."

One of the large monitors shifted to the video image of a man's face, to audible gasps from the crew, as he didn't look much like a man at all. Through clear molecular manipulation, he was pale, bald, and had a face that looked more like a lion's; his nose was thick and pronounced, ears pointed, teeth sharp.

"Do you believe in God, the Planner, the Plan?" the lion-man asked.

"Say nothing!" Calef said, jumping over his father.

"Of course I do," Will answered. "This entire ship does. We have dedicated the lives that God has given us to Him and Him alone." The crew stood strong, some hollering and giving a round of applause.

"My name is Darius," the lion-man replied, "and I am happy to be the one to end your fairy tale." His feed went black.

The Sea Eagle violently shook to the effects of several laser cannon shots, sending a handful of crew members to the floor.

"What's happening?" Will asked.

"You stupid pieces of shit," Alva said. "This is all your fault."

"Where are your guns?" Calef asked.

Joe explained that the Sea Eagle was equipped with three separate laser cannon stations: a large one on the top of the honeycomb-shaped ship called the Beak, and two smaller ones on each of the lower-angled sides called the Talon I and Talon II, which were the right and left side, respectively.

"We're heading for the Beak," Calef told his father, sprinting off with Joan, Rebecca and Alva close behind.

"Joe," Will said, "how many of them are there?"

Joe, the same soldier who accompanied the party that recruited Calef, was the tactical expert on board. He was scanning a large radar at his station.

"They're smart, I'll give them that," he said. "They have some kind of cloaking tech. It's not perfect. I can see ships coming in and out. But I would guess there's at least six of them out there. Let's try to get some cams on them."

On one of the large video screens, smaller feeds started to appear, representing different camera angles outside the ship. The Neo Atheists had patience to match their intelligence; they had waited for the Sea Eagle to enter a heavily clouded patch of air, which obscured their view considerably.

One of the Neo Atheist ships came suddenly into view. Depending on its angle, it was yellow or appeared to reflect no color at all. It was a drone, with four identical engines at its corners, but it was large enough to comfortably fit a human pilot and a passenger. It blasted the Sea Eagle twice before disappearing back in the clouds.

"Damn it," Will said.

"They're called Wasps," a voice said through a speaker at Joe's station. It was Calef reporting from the Beak. "They're just like the bug: fast, scary and annoying as hell."

"We can't help you much with the cams, Calef," Joe told him. "You're going to have to rely on what you can see from the Beak."

"I figured as much," Calef replied. "Can the Talons hear me down below?"

"They can," Joe confirmed.

"Your instinct will be to aim for the center, because that's where the pilot is, but the cockpits are heavily shielded. If you can destroy just one of their engines, the whole thing will fall from the sky. Consider those the wings of a hornet; clip one and the bug can't fly."

"You heard him," Joe said. "It won't be as easy to hit those smaller targets, but that's how we take them out."

Before Joe could end his sentence, three Wasps appeared from underneath, firing as many times as they could at both Talons. The Talons were not ready. Screams burst from the speaker. The Sea

Eagle dropped fifty meters, collectively turning the crew's stomachs.

"Is everyone okay?" Joe asked.

"Talon I is inoperative," a weak voice reported.

"All cannons in Talon I are down?" Joe asked.

"Affirmative," the voice replied.

"Call medics down to Talon I," Joe told Ada.

"On it," she confirmed.

Up in the Beak, Calef was telling the shooters to remain alert, while sitting behind a laser cannon himself. Joan was by his side; Rebecca and Alva stood close together, scanning the clouded sky through the large windows above them.

"There," Rebecca said, pointing off to a corner of cloud that seemed to be stirring and peeling back.

"Got it," Calef said, blasting shot after shot, revealing a Wasp with a blown engine that sank past their view. The Beak crew cheered.

"Shut the fuck up," Alva said. "There's at least five more of them out there, you fucking idiots."

The crew of the Talon I were being evacuated down below, while Talon II waited silently for their turn at another shot.

It came.

The same three Wasps from the last wave started firing from directly below. The Talon II shooters responded in kind, ready this time, taking out the engines of two of the Wasps, which slowed their ascents until they stopped, falling backwards through the clouds and towards the ocean far below.

The Talon II cheered the success on their part, and Alva's voice could be heard over the speaker saying, "They know how stupid they sound, right?"

"That should be half of them, per my estimates," Joe said.

"Your conservative estimates," Calef added.

Both the Beak and Talon II crews gripped the controls of their laser cannons and waited. Calef's palms were raining, and he wiped them on Joan's fur alternately. A few nerve-frying minutes burned past. The only sound echoing through the Sea Eagle was its people breathing heavily, in and out, soon at the same time.

They heard it before they saw it.

Four ships came from the front of the Sea Eagle, tightly together, all firing at the Talon II below. More screams and swears blasted through the communications channel.

"That's seven!" Calef counted, to Joe's annoyed acknowledgment.

"Talon II is down!" a voice conceded.

"What are we supposed to do?" Will asked. "How can we stop them if we can't fight back?"

"How good of a pilot are you, Joe?" Calef asked. Joe smiled.

"Why do you ask?"

"Because I have a feeling you're a damn good one and we could use you right now," Calef said.

"What are you thinking?" Joe asked.

"Everyone on board needs to strap in, now," Calef said. "You're going to spin us around and give the Beak a shot at wherever those Wasps go."

Joe didn't need another word. He nodded to Ada.

"Emergency lockdown," Ada announced over the ship's general communication system. "Effective immediately, get your asses tied down."

Joe walked over to the piloting system and took a seat. He activated the manual controls, while the crew scrambled to find their places.

"You ready, Calef?" Joe asked.

"Let's go," he replied.

Joe sped the Sea Eagle up and started weaving back and forth. The four remaining Wasps started to catch up, revealing parts of themselves through the cottony wisps on either side. Joe turned the ship ninety degrees, giving the Beak a fair shot at two Wasps, whose engines they took out on sheer surprise alone. The two remaining Wasps fell back.

"Do a barrel roll!" Alva shouted.

"Don't do that," Calef said.

Joe instead righted the ship, and then slowed down considerably. A few more moments passed, and they started to wonder if they had retreated. Instead, Joe noticed a quick glitch on his radar.

"One of them has attached to our hull," he said.

"I can't believe I'm going to say this," Calef said, "but do a barrel roll!"

Joe yanked the controls all the way to the right, and the Sea Eagle started spinning, creating a g-force so strong the Wasp lost its grip and was flung to the blue waves below.

"There's still one more," Calef said as the Sea Eagle balanced its way back.

"Another call incoming," Ada said.

"Send them through," Will said.

Darius was back on their screen.

"As long as you hold on to your dangerous beliefs and are a threat to our planet, I will be here to end you. This is far from over."

The screen went black again, and the crew of the Sea Eagle let out a collective sigh.

5

"Dude," said the young man sitting next Calef, clutching his laser cannon controls. "You were awesome. I never want to do that again, but you were awesome."

"What's your name?" Calef asked.

"Hype," he answered.

"That your given name?" Calef asked.

"No, man," Hype said, laughing. His peach cheeks blushed as he put his hands through his thick, white hair. "They call me that because I'm always hyping people up. Or because I'm hyper. Or both."

"Nice to meet you, Hype," Calef said, extending his fist for a bump.

"You're Abe's son, right?" he asked.

"Right," Calef said. "I should go check on him."

"Yeah," he said. "I'll just be here trying to talk myself out of this heart attack."

Calef chuckled as he got up.

"You good, girl?" he asked Joan, who managed to find space under Calef's seat to keep herself secure during the fight. She stretched all the way out and yawned. He scratched her with both hands behind her neck.

"We're fine, too, asshole," Alva said, Rebecca smiling behind him. She ran up and gave Calef a tight hug. Alva subtly averted his eyes, pretending to look for damage done to the Beak.

"Whoa, I'm okay," Calef said.

"That hug was for saving our butts," she said.

"Nothing to it," Calef said with false modesty. "Just another Tuesday." Alva pretended to throw up in his mouth. Calef threw up his hands to faux box him. Alva gripped one of his fists and pulled him in for a hug, too.

They had barely returned to the Chest and caught their breath when Abe met them. Will was still in the middle of the Chest, talking to some of the crew, thanking Joe for his superior flying skills.

"You should go say hi to your siblings before the rest of the sky falls on us," Abe said, half-jokingly.

"That's a good idea," Calef said. "You two going to be okay without me?"

Rebecca and Alva nodded. They headed back to their cabins. Calef and Joan went the opposite way, towards the hall where his family was staying.

Calef had two siblings, both younger: Megan, his sister, was 6 years younger than him, 26 to his 32. Isaac, his brother, had originally come into the world as Issa, his sister. Issa became Isaac at 16, and

Isaac was 22 now. Both shared Calef's dark skin, which they got from their father; their mother, who had passed away when Calef was 18, had a lighter complexion. Maria glowed because, as Abe often said, "she was our angel."

Calef knew it wouldn't be easy to see either of them. It had been 14 years since their mother had died, and Abe had decided to pick up his entire family and move them to Flora.

Except for Calef. Calef stayed behind.

They still remained in contact, albeit through a lukewarm connection. Months, sometimes years, would pass before one would call the other. More often it was a sibling checking in on Calef, especially in those early years. But sometimes Calef would make the video call.

Most of the time they would end in stand offs, or standoffish goodbyes.

But he loved them, unconditionally, sometimes in spite of their conditions.

He approached Megan's cabin first.

"Knock, knock," he said aloud.

"Brother!" Megan said, rushing into him, splashing in his arms, dancing side to side, her brown hair bouncing up and down.

"Christmas came early?" he joked.

"Here, it's Christmas all the time," she pointed out.

"True, true," he said. "I wish it didn't take a world-changing prophecy for us to get together."

"You don't believe it?" she asked.

"What do you think?" he asked back.

"I think you're just as stubborn as ever, brother," she said. There was a long pause. It was painful for the both of them.

"Let's not get into this," he said.

"Why?" she asked.

"We've had this conversation," he said. "We always have this conversation. I look into your eyes, and I see you looking at me like everyone else here looks at me. I can feel you feeling sorry for me."

"I just . . ." she started, then tears filled her eyes. "I just don't get why you wouldn't want to see mom again in Heaven."

"Why the fuck wouldn't I want that?" he asked. "Of course I want that. All I want is to see mom again, Meg. But it's not real. And I have to find hope here, sister. If I don't, then I don't see a life worth living."

She slid her hand under her nose, sniffling. She rubbed the bridge of Joan's nose, up and down, before coming back in for another hug.

"Isaac is having a hard time," she said, quietly. "He pretends that he isn't, but he is."

"I'll talk to him," Calef said.

"He's not the problem," she said.

"I know," he said. With that, he kissed his sister on the head and went across the hall to see his brother. The door was shut.

"Hey, baby brother," Calef said. "Can we come in?"

"Of course," Isaac said from behind the door, swinging it open and squeezing Calef as hard as he could. "I missed you. So much."

"I missed you, too," Calef said, putting his hand behind his brother's short, thick hair. "That's a hell of a mustache."

"Isn't it?" Isaac said, using his finger as a comb. "I am quite the ladies man on Flora."

"I'm glad I don't have to compete with you on this planet," Calef said, putting Isaac into a playful headlock. Isaac pulled right out of it, wrapping his arms around Calef from behind. Joan barked for Calef's freedom, before he declared: "You win!"

They laughed and Isaac turned back into his room.

"You still like coffee?" Isaac asked.

"Like it? It's my life blood," Calef replied. Isaac used a voice command to start his coffee maker.

"I have five different regions of coffee with me," he said. "Do you have a preference?"

"I don't know much about the regional differences of the coffee on Flora, you snob," Calef said as he playfully punched Isaac on the arm. "Surprise me."

So Isaac did, preparing a cup of coffee so damn good that Calef had to begrudgingly admit: "Okay, that is pretty damn good." They talked for a little while longer, and Calef could sense what his sister told him. It broke his heart. But Calef, stubborn big brother, was determined to fix it.

He would be of service in any way he could.

. . .

Alva walked into his cabin. Rebecca followed him in.

"Your cabin is over there," Alva said, pointing across the hall.

"But I want to hang out with you," she said.

"Why?" he asked.

"Why are you like this?" she asked back.

"I don't know what you mean," he said, averting his eyes from hers, trying to press down his smile, trying to push down those things called feelings.

"You like me," she declared. "I like you. Say it back."

"You're insane," he said. "You are an insane woman."

"Why is that crazy?" she asked.

"We're friends," he said. "And we're both friends with Calef."

"What does he have to do with anything?" she asked, genuinely confused.

"You two are closer than anyone I know," Alva said, now displaying a rare case of vulnerability. "It's hard to watch."

"So, would it surprise you to know that Calef and I have only ever been friends, only want to be friends, and will forever only be friends?"

Alva looked unconvinced.

"I know some people don't think it's possible," she continued. "But two extremely attractive people can be friends. Calef and I are the extremely attractive people I'm talking about here."

"I got that."

"Okay, good," she said. "I love Calef. He's my best friend. But there is something missing from us that we're just never going to have, and we both know it. We've talked about it. I'm sorry if that's uncomfortable for you to think about, but it's true. You and I, on the other hand – you know, maybe I'm out of line."

Alva said nothing, his eyes still fixated on the ground.

"Yeah," she said. "Maybe I just read this wrong."

Wordlessly, Rebecca walked across the hall into her own cabin.

. . .

Calef was walking back to find his father when he felt a pair of eyes on him, and tried to play aloof as he felt tingling wave after tingling wave wash across his body. He turned to see Maya smiling at him from a doorway towards the back of the Chest. She had two cups in her hand.

"Coffee?" she asked.

"I just had one," he answered.

"That isn't a no," she countered.

"No arguments here," he said.

They found a small table in the corner of the dining hall to sit. At first, they said nothing. But neither could stop smiling.

"Come here often?" he asked.

"Oh, that's bad," she said. "I'm guessing you're single."

"That is a very astute observation, as my friend Rebecca would say," he said. "She is my friend. Rebecca. Is my friend."

"I'm not worried either way," Maya said.

It had been so long since Calef had flirted with a woman that he wasn't sure what flirting back sounded like. Was she just being friendly? Was he reading too far into this? Was he already into her? Was he so damn shallow?

"I just have to tell you this upfront, I'm not religious," he said, hoping not to dampen what he felt were sparks.

"Why would I assume you were?" she asked.

"Have you met my dad?" he said.

"Yeah, and he's religious enough for the both of you," she said, and they laughed together.

"I think he thinks if he believes hard enough, he can get me into Heaven, too," Calef said, his smile softening. "Like a two-for-one soul deal."

"So you believe in a soul?" she asked.

"I do, but I have a complicated relationship with the word *soul*," he said.

"Do tell," she said.

"Well," he started, "*soul* is a word that doesn't actually mean anything. Like, if I say orange, you think of the color, or the fruit. It describes something that exists. There is no definitive measure of a soul, and everyone seems to have a different definition for it. And there are a lot of words like that. *God. Devil.* But if the words make you feel something when you hear them, they then become real themselves, because they have real effects."

"I'm following, but this is a hell of rabbit hole we're tumbling down," she said.

"The problem is when we use words that don't exist to affect things that do. For example, there would be no abortion debate if we didn't believe in souls. We think that as soon as a sperm fertilizes an egg, a soul is put in there, too. That is the only reason we could think fetuses are fully realized human beings."

Maya couldn't believe this man thought this was flirting. He went on.

"Can you imagine if I took two pieces of thread, made two stitches with them and then told you that was a hat? That is not a hat, not any more than an egg/sperm collision is a human being that can think and feel and play the guitar."

"So do you think abortion is murder?" she asked.

"Is it murder to pull the plug on a man who has no chance of ever recovering the use of his brain?" he asked in return. "A lot of people, myself included, think animals have souls, but don't have a problem killing them. Is ending any life we consider to have a soul in any way murder?"

"I don't know," she said. "But can you keep a secret?"

"Sure," he said.

"I'm not strictly a Christian," she admitted. "There are things I like. I'm a big fan of Jesus and that Christ-like lifestyle. But I'm the kind of person who likes to use any tool that works. And sometimes those come from a different box. I think you and I might be the same like that."

And like that, Calef was in love.

. . .

"What's the plan when we get to the site?" Joe asked.

"The plan hasn't changed," Will said. They both quietly sputtered, their words getting just enough mileage to reach each other's ears.

"You don't think Calef and his pals are going to be trouble?" Joe asked.

"No," Will said.

"They're smart."

"I know."

"They could figure it out."

"I know."

"They could talk."

"And nobody would listen," Will said, putting a nail in their conversation. "You and I are the only two people on this ship with the clearance to know the truth about the asteroid site and the phoenix. Let's proceed, however, like we don't. Are we clear?"

"As the water on Flora," Joe said as Will walked away.

. . .

"You did good today, son," Abe said, after spotting Calef and Maya bonding over a cup of coffee in the dining room. "I'm proud of you."

"Thanks, dad," he said, looking over at Maya, not wanting this conversation to end but, inspired, knowing there was another one he had to start. "Will you excuse me, Maya? I have to speak to my father for a minute."

Calef left the table and caught up with his dad, who had already made it back into the Chest.

"Can we talk real quick, dad?" Calef asked.

"Of course," Abe said.

"It's about Isaac," Calef said.

"Oh," Abe said.

"God doesn't make mistakes, son," Will chimed in from a few meters away. "Issa is mistaken in thinking that body wasn't made for her."

A raw heat vented out of Calef.

"Excuse me?" Calef said. "I don't remember saying a goddamn thing to you. And if you call me 'son' or 'boy' again, I'll show you what I can do to your God-given body. I will remake you in my image."

"Your temper, son," Abe reminded him.

"No," Calef said. "I'm talking for a moment. On behalf of my *brother*. For *Isaac*."

"There is nothing you can say that can change my mind," Will said.

"I don't give a shit about your old, ignorant, white-guy brain," Calef said. "People like you will die soon enough. No, I need to speak to my father's heart, about his son."

"Say your peace," Abe said.

"Dad, do you believe in a soul?" Calef asked.

By this time, Calef's outburst had attracted several onlookers. The crew was listening to this conversation, and Abe had fallen silent.

"I didn't think this was a hard question," Calef said. "Do you believe in a soul?"

"Of course I do," Abe said.

"Do you think a soul has a gender?" Calef asked.

Abe was dumbfounded. He didn't know how to answer the question.

"We made up gender," Calef went on. "We decided how a girl looks and how a boy looks, how a girl acts and how a boy acts, what a girl can do and what a boy can do, but the thing to remember is: we made it all up. Like words. Like race. We needed a way to easily recognize power, and what's more easy than splitting us up as white and brown and black folks?"

The assembled crew looked mostly uncomfortable, but as Rebecca liked to say, truth was in the uncomfortable.

"Look, no matter what any one of you believes in here, we are all made up of the same matter," Calef continued. "This coffee cup I'm holding is made up as the same stuff as you and I are, and it's the same stuff that makes up stars and snow and Neo Atheists. To assume that the stuff we're made of is who we are goes against the very idea of a soul. So, I'm going to ask you again, father: do you think a soul has a gender?"

"I . . . I don't know," Abe said.

Calef looked to the other side of the Chest, and saw that Isaac was standing against the wall. He smiled at Calef, his thumb under his chin, combing his mustache with his finger.

"I hate to break up this emotional family moment," Joe said, breathlessly. "But the Sea Eagle is going down. Right now."

6

"That's a little dramatic, I'm sorry," Joe clarified. "What I meant is, we're almost over Australia and we have to land the Sea Eagle immediately to repair the Talons."

Several sighs of relief were released, some from the confrontation that had just occurred, and others from the realization that they were not going to die. Joe was correct on two matters, though: the Sea Eagle had just about made it to Australia, and they needed to fix their lower weapons systems immediately.

"There are threats in Australia that we are not currently equipped to handle if we encounter them," Joe said. "We've considered that some of the reports may be just exaggerated rumors, like the potential threat of a comically named terrorist called the Cosmic Kangaroo, but we need to err on the safe side. We will be grounding the Sea Eagle on the coast of Brisbane, which is just a few hours east of the asteroid impact site in Toowoomba. We'll have to assemble a party to reach the site via hovermobiles, while a team repairs the ship on the ground."

Calef's ears perked up at the mention of hovermobiles. Smaller vehicles that had been previously known as snowmobiles, motorcycles and jet skis, but now retrofitted with hover tech, hovermobiles were fast, highly maneuverable and, honestly, a lot of fun. While hovercars and spaceships were great advancements in getting people from place to place, nothing matched the feeling of getting behind a hovermobile and just going.

Joe immediately started to assemble the site team. Since Rebecca had made it part of their deal, she, Alva and Calef (along with Joan) were already on the roster, as were Will, Abe and his son, Isaac. Joe's good friend, Jan, a member of the science team, had asked to accompany them and Joe couldn't have been happier.

"Is there anyone else you think would be good on this trip?" Joe asked Calef.

"There was this guy up in the Beak with me, Hype, I think?" said Calef.

"Yeah, he's a good kid," Joe said. "I'll add him."

"Do you really think you're doing this without me?" a voice behind Calef said. He turned around to see Maya, finishing her coffee and tossing the cup in the recycling bin.

"I wouldn't dare," Calef said, and then turned to Joe. "She's my plus-one, I guess."

"Someone's gotta protect your ass," Maya said.

"I have Joan," Calef said, letting the Golden Saint lick his hand. She gave Maya a jealous glare, her eyes fixed, Maya's look locked.

"Someone's gotta protect *both* your asses," Maya said. "Look at that good girl. She wouldn't hurt a tick."

Maya called Joan's bluff. Joan approached her for immediate petting.

"Okay, that's ten, plus Joan," Joe said. "I think we have at least a dozen hovermobiles onboard so that's more than enough."

"I'll go let my friends know," Calef said. He smiled at Maya. "See you out there?"

"It's a date," she said.

. . .

Calef and Joan knocked on Rebecca's cabin door.

"Fuck off," she said.

"Wait, what?" Calef asked.

"Oh!" she said, running to open it. "Sorry. I thought you two were someone else."

"A Jehovah's witness?" he asked.

"Alva," she said.

"Is everything okay?" he asked.

"It's fine," she sighed. "What's up?

"We're landing in just a minute," he said. "Ten of us make up the survey party and we're taking hovermobiles to the site in Toowoomba."

"Hovermobiles?" she said. "Fuck yes."

"Right?" he agreed. "Even Joan is excited." Joan enthusiastically barked.

"I'll go get Alva and we'll meet in the Chest," she said.

"You don't want me to talk to him?" he asked.

"I don't run away from my problems, Calef," she said. "I face them blue-head on. I'll get him."

Calef and Joan left. Rebecca knocked on Alva's door. He answered apprehensively.

"Let's go," she said.

Alva wasn't sure what was going to be colder: the impending journey, or Rebecca herself.

. . .

The survey team gathered by the elevator in the Chest: Calef, Joan, Rebecca, Alva, Maya, Joe, Jan, Hype, Abe, Isaac and Will. Under their outdoor gear, each member was wearing laser-proof material, which was good at stopping laser fire, but not perfect or permanent through persistent blasts. Each person was also equipped with a large backpack full of supplies and one lasergun. Laserguns needed no ammunition; they were powered by a reactor, which did need time to reenergize, but not reload. The entire crew of the Sea Eagle was gathered around to hear the plan.

"Our goal is simple," Will said. "We are here to survey the asteroid site, which no one from Flora has been personally able to do. We're to take a variety of readings, photos, and samples from the site, including the extraction of soil and rocks. The radiation report says that we are safe to enter, but we still don't want to court any risk, so we will be efficient and do this as quickly as possible. I'll turn it over to Calef to tell us what we should do if we encounter any more Neo Atheists."

"The simplest way to avoid conflict with a Neo Atheist is to say nothing at all," Calef said. "You heard what Darius asked: 'Do you believe in God, the Planner, the Plan?' That is their test. If you do not engage, they will find it harder to justify their violence. That isn't to say they won't still attack you. But denying their question could save your life."

"What if I refuse to refuse my Lord?" Will asked.

"Then they'll try to kill you," Calef said. "It's simple."

"Then maybe that would justify my violence," Will said. "Maybe I wouldn't mind killing a few Neo Atheists while I'm down here." A few of the crew vocalized their support of that idea.

"That's great," Calef said, "because if you're willing to admit that you believe in a god, a god that has demanded and encouraged murder and genocide on this planet countless times, then they wouldn't mind killing you either."

"Don't you mean *the* God?" Will asked.

"I do not," Calef answered.

There was some chatter among the crew. Some were clearly not impressed with Calef or his attitude.

"These people are just as dangerous as any extremist," Calef continued. "Some Neo Atheists are so extreme that they'll even kill an agnostic, like myself, or any person who doesn't definitively refuse any kind of divine power."

"Can I ask you a question?" Jan said. This was the first time Calef had heard her talk. She was a large figure, with short, wavy gray hair; her physicality was imposing, but her eyes could not have been more kind. "How do you know so much about Neo Atheists?"

Calef shared a look of regret with his father.

"I used to be one," Calef answered. "When my mother died, and my family left and moved to Flora, I was lost. I was looking for a home, and one of the places I looked was with the Neo Atheists. It didn't take long for me to realize they were not my kind. I never murdered anybody. But I didn't stop anyone, either."

There were audible gasps from the crew. Most of them were shocked, but a few felt a sense of awe and curiosity about Calef and his past. A few more already knew, like his friends, family, and Will.

"It's not an easy part of my life to talk about," he said. "But I will, if anyone has questions. I feel like being open about it helps me understand it, and helps people understand me."

"We can ask questions later," Will said. "Time is of the essence, and we must go."

The asteroid site team assembled on the elevator. It began its descent, and stopped on the dark level below the deck of the Chest. The room illuminated, revealing that it was a garage filled with vehicles, mostly hovermobiles. Calef spotted his ride immediately.

It had been an all-black jet ski decades ago. The seat was designed to fit at least three humans, which would be more than enough room for him and Joan. There was a thick, black blanket tied to the back, which would be the perfect tarp to shield her from the wind.

"This is the one," he said to her and smiled. He put on the helmet that was sitting on the seat and turned the hovermobile on. It hummed, floating half a meter off the ground. Joan jumped on back, creating a nest under the tarp.

Four hovermobiles at a time, they were lowered down the elevator to the outside world. It was windy, and cold; nothing new. When eight vehicles were on the ground, just Calef and Rebecca were left in the garage.

"Should we go for it?" she asked.

"You know me too well," he said.

Instead of waiting for the elevator to come back and pick them up, they launched themselves out the open door, surprising the rest of the team below. Laughing, they took off full speed towards Toowoomba, the others eating their snow dust while trying to catch up.

7

They were cruising over the open, snowy Australian plain. Specks of snow fell from the sky and sped past their eyes like warped shooting stars. The sun was out in all her glory today, burning hot against a gray gradient sky but getting low; the wind was to their back, and made their travel easier, if not almost comfortable.

The temperature of the planet rarely rose above freezing, but even a few degrees below that number could feel like a dream. Everything is relative, and appreciation is only as useful as the person who wields it, which was something the people of Earth knew far better than the people of Flora.

The helmets of the team were connected through an integrated audio system; they could address the whole team or individuals using voice commands.

"I'm looking at our current scans," Jan said to the entire crew, "and I'm seeing trouble up ahead. Outdated maps marked this trip as taking a little over an hour; there are asteroid-made canyons up ahead, and we're going to have to slow down significantly when we reach them."

This news unsettled the asteroid team. Time was a concern, as was the possibility of not making it to the site and back before the sun went down.

"I think it's cool that you were able to turn your life around," a voice said to Calef's ear. It was Hype on a direct feed.

"Thanks, man," Calef said. He turned his head over to Hype and nodded.

"People are so concerned with boxes, you know?" Hype said. "They meet you, and you're one thing, so they think you're that one thing for the rest of your life. They forget that everything is just changing all the time, including people. There are no boxes. There's just you and me and nothing in between."

"I couldn't agree more," Calef said.

"Just keep being honest," Hype said. "Fuck the haters."

"Fuck the haters," Calef said.

The site team rode for another half hour in radio silence. It was nice to be out of the ship. In the distance, they could start to see the rising rocks of the canyons.

"Can we go around, Jan?" Joe asked, addressing the team.

"Not really," Jan said. "The canyons extend completely around the blast range. There may be easier paths to navigate, but we'll be going through these rocks all the same."

Jan took the lead, leaning left to drive the crew towards the most open trail she could find in their immediate view.

"We should be able to fit two hovermobiles side-by-side through here, but that's it," Jan said. "That's how narrow this path is, and it's crooked and jagged and angry with rocks and ice."

They started to slow as they approached the mouth of the canyon road. Calef retook the lead, followed by the rest, with Joe bringing up the rear. The stony sides extended hundreds of meters upwards; some of the walls were flat all the way to the top, while others had cliffs and ledges protruding from their faces.

Every movement echoed through the asteroid-made valley. Calef took off his helmet, and the rest of the team followed his lead.

"This is fucking spooky," Alva said.

"Don't run away now," Rebecca said. Alva forcefully blew air out of his nose.

"Something feels weird," Joe said to Jan. "Do you feel it?"

"Yeah," Jan said, and then pointed up. "Do those look like caves in the walls?"

They fell back, not stopping but trolling, to take a better look.

"Avoiding me?" Maya asked Calef, pulling up to his hovermobile.

"Not at all," Calef said. "Though I can imagine you probably see me differently now."

"Not at all," Maya said. "I try not make to assumptions, but when I first saw you, I thought I was looking at a broken man who had managed to put himself back together."

Calef pressed his lips together, frowning slightly.

"I'm happy to say that I don't think I was wrong," Maya finished.

"It's nice of you to say that," Calef said.

"Now, what did you think when you first saw me?" Maya asked with a self-serving grin.

A sharp sound. Smoke jumping from a wall.

"That's a laser shot," Joe said. "We're not alone."

Calef looked up to see four people with concealed faces on various cliffs, holding laserguns pointed in their direction. The masks they hid under were made of shiny black material, resembling opaque face shields with two large circular indents where eyes should be. They appeared to work in the same manner as one-way mirrors. One of them pulled off his mask, revealing a face that was half-human, half-marsupial.

"Do you believe in God, the Planner, the Plan?" the Cosmic Kangaroo asked. Joe couldn't believe his eyes.

Calef put his hand out flat, signaling to his team to not engage. They sat there in silence.

"Your quiet is not an answer," he said.

"We do not," Calef said. "We are just people of this secular world seeking passage through this canyon."

The marsupial-man appeared satisfied by his answer, but the laserguns did not go down. Calef swallowed hard but remained stoic. Nobody moved, from up above or down below.

But Alva did sense movement. To his right side, he saw an arm being raised. Alva looked over at Minister Will Mather, and watched his hand move up slowly. It touched his head, and then his chest, and then tapped each of his shoulders.

"That man did a sign of worship," the Cosmic Kangaroo said and, now filled with vindictive venom, spit.

"*Goddamn it*, Will," Alva said. "What is your fucking problem?"

Laser blasts rained upon the team.

"Go!" Joe yelled.

Calef pushed his helmet back on, the rest of the crew following suit, and then started navigating the canyon floor as quickly and as carefully as he could. He pulled out his own lasergun and tried to return fire blindly, driving one-handed and unable to take his eyes off the perilous path. The team members adept at using laserguns were doing the same: returning fire and avoiding collision.

The helmets were designed to dispel lasers, as were the hovermobiles themselves. The tarp covering Joan was made of the same material their laser-proof vests were. These precautions helped as they took blast after blast, but the sheer force of the laser power was brutal in itself, and no shielding could stop that.

A scream was heard towards the back of their pack.

Calef turned around to see Rebecca on her back in the snow, her hovermobile completely on fire, crashed into a large boulder.

"Rebecca!" Alva called before Calef could. Alva turned his hovermobile around to pick her up. The Neo Atheists now all focused their shots on him.

"Cover him!" Calef commanded. The team stopped driving forward to focus all their attention on providing laser fire to help Alva. Their low ground was making it near impossible to take a shot that connected; the Neo Atheists knew their power in the high ground and were fearless in their actions.

Alva took shot after shot, and the physical toll was quickly adding up. The Cosmic Kangaroo realized that he had gotten caught up in the moment; the better target would be the girl on her back in the snow. He changed his aim. He lowered his lasergun carefully. He smiled, content in his belief that he was fighting the good fight on behalf of nature itself.

"Whoo hoo!" an unfamiliar female voice laughed, echoing through all ears. A shadow jumped over the gap, cool colors rippling in the light.

The laser fire that Neo Atheists used was generally red, as that was the natural color of heat. The Knight's laser fire was yellow, the golden color of the sun and Heaven. Blue blasts started shooting across the canyon, over the site team's heads. There was someone else up there. One of the Neo Atheists yelled, and then his body fell off a ridge and onto the ground in front of them, his mask cracked in half.

Alva was finally able to get to Rebecca. He carefully picked her up and put her on the back of his hovermobile.

"Not running away from you this time," he said to her. "Running with you."

The rest of the crew was trying to figure out what was happening. There was clearly another contender up there, someone who was not on the side of the Atheists. She had taken out one, but there was still at least three to deal with. The laser fire started to die down, with a few red blasts here matched by a few blue there, until there was none.

A roar.

A hovermobile, formally a blue motorcycle with comically large handlebars, drove off a cliff above. It landed in front of the team. On the bike was a woman, wearing a white, hooded poncho. Her exposed face was almost as pale, sprinkled with light freckles, and she was wrapped in a gray scarf tucked underneath her coat.

"Howdy, y'all," she said.

"Who are you?" Calef asked, lasergun pointed.

"I'm called the Loner," she said. "I'll help you get out of here."

"Why should we trust you?" Will asked.

"Because no matter how much you hate them Neo Atheists, I hate them more," she said.

That answer satisfied Calef, and he followed her, the rest of the crew closely behind him.

"We need to move fast," she said. "My guess is they're going back to base to bring more of them here." She wove between the rocks like floss, which both impressed and challenged Calef.

"What brought you to us?" he asked.

"I was tracking them," she said. "I thought they caught on, got spooked, but it turned out you set off one of their alarms, and they came running."

"You from around here?" he asked.

"Am not," she said. "I go where they go. I've got a tab to settle. Stop."

She came to an abrupt halt. The rest of the team stopped, too, unsure of her and her reasons. They could feel it before they heard it. Vibrations in the wind. Then the rumble became audible and panic set in.

"I was wrong," she said.

"About what?" Calef asked.

"They didn't go back," she said. "I know what's coming."

"You want to share with the class, cowgirl?" Alva asked.

"They set up a trap," she said. "Damn it. Stupid. I saw them fenced in half a kilometer away."

"Saw who fenced in?" Calef asked. She shook her head.

"There's a herd of mammoths heading this way."

8

Will couldn't have heard that right.

"Excuse me?" he said.

"Mammoths," the Loner repeated. "Big, furry elephants. Is he a bit slow?"

"He is," Alva confirmed.

"But how is that possible?" Will asked. "Mammoths don't exist."

"I'm not sure what you mean," the Loner said. "They're here so they exist."

"DNA tech has come a long way," Calef said. "Most of the children born here, myself and my siblings included, have the Viking DNA mod. It makes our bodies more adaptable to cold temperatures. You may have noticed the distinctive facial features some of the Neo Atheists have. Those are DNA mods, too. Atheists have been becoming more animal-like over generations, in their attempt to live more in accordance with nature."

"I know about DNA mods," Will said. "We use them on Flora, too. But I thought mammoths were a myth. One of those conspiracies the less-intelligent Earthers believed, like that their own planet is flat, or the Velos asteroid was created by the government. What does DNA have to do with mammoths?"

"Once we fully understood DNA," Calef said. "We became God."

"We don't have time for this," the Loner said. "My plan was to lead you out of here, but we won't make it before the mammoths do. I have a secret cave up ahead. If we hurry, we won't die to death."

She started ahead, the team close behind. But no matter how close they stayed, how elegantly they avoided the nasty edges of rock and ice, the rumbling grew, the noise intensified. Minutes passed and it felt like the mammoths were on top of them, but they had yet to make themselves seen.

The sound of thunder. The forceful shifting of earth. What had started as a drizzle of pebbles was escalating into the downfall of stones, and now an entire cliff had cracked off the canyon wall.

"Hurry!" the Loner said.

They rushed to get ahead of the impending landslide. One by one they passed under the noise, now akin to the crunch of bones breaking, until they all had made it through and the ledge crashed down behind them.

"Will that stop the mammoths?" Will asked.

"Only long enough to piss them off," the Loner said.

She was right. Will turned around and saw one for the first time. Thick hair and strong teeth and massive feet. Tusks bursting through frozen earth. The landslide wasn't a blockade for them; it was an annoyance.

"How close are we to the cave?" Calef asked.

"Close enough, I hope," the Loner said.

They continued to move as fast as they could over the narrow earthquake zone. The Loner's eyes were darting up and down the right side of the canyon.

"What are you looking for?" Calef asked.

"A piece of my gray scarf," she said. "I stuck it between the rock I put in front of the entrance."

"It's back there," a weak voice said from behind the pack. It was Rebecca. "I tried to say something, but it's so loud. I saw the scarf. It's a hundred meters back."

"Towards the mammoths?" Will asked.

"Go!" the Loner commanded.

The team reversed their motion and their order, now running backwards towards the stampede of wooly mammoths. The mammoths had broken through the fallen cliff now and were getting back up to speed.

"There!" the Loner said, pointing at a small piece of cloth sticking out of the canyon wall. Joe and Jan jumped off their hovermobiles and started pushing the massive rock covering the entrance. It started to slowly roll over. The mammoths were less than three hundred meters away.

"How did you push this by yourself?" Joe asked, grunting as he threw all his weight behind the door.

"I pulled it over with my bike," she said. Alva joined Joe and Jan and they all took a step a back, counted to three, and pushed the boulder at the same time. It rolled all the way forward, revealing a massive hideout within. One by one, they drove their hovermobiles inside, the Loner just barely getting hers over the threshold before the first mammoths went screaming past.

"Mammoths," Abe said, smiling, simply unable to believe his eyes.

. . .

A few hours passed and it was dark outside.

Mammoths weren't running by anymore. Some were still walking past, trying to figure the best way out. Others had given up, lying down and waiting for the dawn, or something worse.

"We should probably do the same," the Loner said, pointing to a sleeping Mammoth completely blocking their way out.

They built a fire.

Earlier, Will had contacted the Sea Eagle and updated them on their progress, or lack thereof now. The good news back from the ship was that it would be fully repaired by morning, and able to pick up the team from the asteroid site. They would only have to make the rest of the journey there.

Most of the team was sitting around the fire, eating food that had been stored in their backpacks. The smell of smoke was thick and rich, the only way for it to leave the sole entrance they used. Rebecca was lying down at the very back of the cave with

Alva and Joan, who were taking care of her. Rebecca's hands were cracked from the cold. Alva opened a tube of Aquafill and rubbed the clear lotion over them. Within seconds, her skin was healed.

"I'm an ass," Alva said quietly.

"I know," Rebecca said.

"I mean, I'm sorry," he said. "About earlier."

"Look, I know you're insecure sometimes," she said. "I get it. I understand that feeling. But it's also not my job to constantly reassure you of things you already know."

"Can you sometimes?" he asked.

"Yeah," she said. "Do you want to know when I knew you could be my person?"

"Sure," he said.

"We were all at the bar late, before you owned it," she said. "A man walked in and he smelled terrible. Like trash."

"Trashy Terry," he said.

"Yeah, Trashy Terry," Rebecca laughed. "Because he smelled like trash. Nobody wanted him there. He sat down at the bar and, right away, these blockheads started teasing him and throwing popcorn at him. You looked over, and one by one, you started roasting those bullies. Just really digging into all their defects and flaws. It was hilarious and mean and raw and perfect in so many ways."

"You liked me because I'm mean?" he asked.

"After they left – thoroughly embarrassed, might I add – you walked over to Terry. You talked to him for a few minutes, and you didn't roll your eyes, and you didn't sigh heavily, but you listened. You bought him a beer and I saw you slide him a few more dollars for whatever he needed."

"He's okay, that Terry," he said. "Still smells like shit."

"Scientist or not, I believe in a soul," she said. "And that night I felt yours touch mine. I've been stuck to it ever since."

Alva put his fingers between Rebecca's and gently squeezed. Joan rested her head on top of their hands.

"Where are you from?" Calef asked the Loner. "You said you weren't from around here earlier."

"America," she said.

"Us, too," he said. "Why are you tracking the Neo Atheists?"

"None of your business," she said. "I'm plain and friendly and all, but I don't know you."

"That's right," he said. "You don't. I'm Calef." He extended his hand. She shook it, and he introduced the rest of the crew, and explained to her why they were there. Will, of course, had his own points to make, but both Calef and Will relented to let Abe describe the prophecy of the Great Lakes phoenix, as Abe seemed to really enjoy telling it.

"You're good people," the Loner said, enjoying some of the dried meat they shared with her. "Some of you might believe in some out there stuff, but you're good people."

They sat in silence a while, the kind of quiet where one gets to know those around them wordlessly.

"I hate them," the Loner finally said. "I know hating is bad. But I really, truly, in my bones, hate them."

They looked at her and understood the feeling she described.

"My wife Molly is the sweetest thing in the world. She wouldn't so much as pinch a snowflake. She is so gentle. She is so kind."

She swallowed hard.

"I say *is* because *was* is so hard to say. They killed her. The Neo Atheists, I mean."

"Was she a believer?" Will asked. The Loner nodded her head.

"Yeah," she said. "Muslim. She loved God so much. She prayed as much as she kissed me. And she kissed me lots."

"Is that why you're tracking them down?" Calef asked. She nodded again.

"I'm looking for the one that did it," she said. "Lion-man named Darius."

They all looked at each other. The Loner noticed.

"We met him," Calef said. "He attacked our ship as soon as we got over the ocean, so he was in America, and my guess is he went back."

"He was here, for a while," she said. "But the trail had got cold, no pun intended, and I had no leads. I guess I met y'all for a reason."

"Are you a believer?" Abe asked.

"Hell, no," the Loner said. "I believe in the here and now. What I can see and taste and smell. And God don't smell like nothing."

Calef got a good laugh out of that.

"I'm going to grab a pop," Hype said to Calef. "Can I grab you one?"

"Sure," he said.

Hype walked over towards the front of the cave. The Loner watched him, and then noticed something.

"I ain't heard nothing in a while," she said.

"What do you mean?" Calef asked.

"No mammoth sounds," she said.

The entrance to the cave had turned completely black, a void. A huge gust of wind blew through, putting out the fire and plunging them into darkness. An unearthly growl permeated the room.

Then a sigh. A gasp. A thud, and a rolling sound.

Calef felt something tap his shoe. He put his hand forward to feel for it. It was warm and round and wet. He got a little closer and he was horrified.

He was looking at Hype's dismembered head.

9

Calef tried to scream but his vocal cords had run completely dry.

"He's dead," he managed to say.

"Who's dead?" a voice in the darkness asked.

"Hype," Calef said. "His head is on the ground."

"Everyone head to the back of the cave," the Loner said in a calm tone. She was determined to keep both her cool and everyone safe.

A hissing sound entered the cave, growing louder and getting softer over the next few minutes. Sometimes it seemed like it was in the cave, sometimes it appeared to be outside. The team was making their way as far back from the entrance as they could. The ceiling seemed to be cracking, as though it was expanding.

"What is it?" Isaac asked. He had been quiet the entire trek, contemplative. Now he, along with everyone else, had the urgent need to know what they were dealing with.

"Leviathan," Will said.

"Stop with the religious bullshit," Alva said.

"It's the truth!" Will said.

"Alva is right, Will," Calef said. "We need to figure out what this really is so we can stop it."

"You're the native, so why don't you tell us?" Will snapped at him.

On any other day, at any given time, Calef would have punched Will right in the face. His concern over the intruder was too great to break his focus. They could hear a slithering creep closer on both sides, the sound of scales scraping against the walls. They were all crowded together now, clutching to each other's legs and arms and hands, packed like peanuts in a jar.

It growled from one direction, and then immediately from another.

"Son," Abe said, "the Leviathan has many heads. Listen."

"It's not the Leviathan!" Calef said.

"The Leviathan has been described as many things," Will said. "Snake. Beast. Dragon."

"It's not a dragon!" Calef said.

"We need to turn on a light," Joe said.

"My hovermobile is back here," Alva said. "I could use its headlight."

Maya felt something move past her leg. Isaac felt the same thing. They started clinging even harder, almost climbing on top of each other. The growling now seemed to be overhead, and straight in front of them at the same time.

"Does anyone have their lasergun on them?" Calef asked.

"I do," Joe said.

"Okay, Alva, count to three and then turn on your light. Joe, get ready to shoot whatever he shows us."

They agreed and Alva sat down on his hovermobile. He started it up, and it made a humming noise that echoed through the cave and irritated the creature that shared it.

"One . . ." Alva started. Joe pulled out his lasergun.

"Two . . ." he continued. Joe aimed forward.

"Three."

Alva turned the light on, illuminating an eyeball over three meters wide.

Joe started firing. The creature howled from several points, and the cave started to quake. Something shattered the headlight of Alva's hovermobile, but Joe kept shooting. Alva revved his engine. The commotion seemed to be driving the creature, or creatures, back.

Joan started barking. Maya jumped in front of her and picked her up, moving her behind all the people.

"I know you're a good girl," Maya said. "But this is not your fight."

Joe sat down on Alva's hovermobile.

"Drive forward," Joe said.

"Are you crazy?" Alva asked. "We can't see anything."

"We have to push it out," Joe said.

Alva did as he was told. Slowly, the hovermobile propelled towards the screaming, snarling beast, Joe relentless in his blasting. In the brief bursts of golden light, they tried to make out what it was. Some saw the snake. Some saw the dragon. Some saw dozens of tentacles. Some saw impossible rows of teeth. Some saw countless heads.

All saw a beast they could not explain.

Finally, the last limbs of the creature left the cave. The team quickly pushed a large boulder in front of the entrance, which had been greatly expanded, leaving a large open gap over the top of the rock. They collapsed in various places around the room, trying to catch their breath. Hype's head was the only part of him that stayed behind, his body nowhere to be found.

Calef, spread out on his back, allowed himself a moment to collect his disparate pieces. He turned his head to Maya.

"If you and I ever go on a date, and then we start going steady, and then we get married, and then we have kids, I will be able to tell them the story of tonight, and how I fell in love with their mom the moment she saved my dog."

"Let's just try to survive tonight," she said.

It was not a peaceful rest.

It was agreed that at least two people at a time would stay awake and take watch, but during any one minute through the night, less than half of the team was asleep. There was the adrenaline and excitement, certainly, but it was mostly fear that kept them from their dreams.

. . .

The sun peeked through the glaring wink over the boulder. Most of the crew was already up. The mood was somber as they wrapped Hype's head in a small blanket, the senseless death not any clearer under the morning light.

The boulder was moved and they assessed the canyon. Blood and mammoth guts covered the walls, but there wasn't a live creature in sight in either direction. Floran coffee was made, and nuts and dried fruit were nibbled on. Appetites were also nowhere to be found.

Calef was having feelings he hadn't felt in a long time, and they were turning his stomach. The way he felt about Maya turned it like a net, trying to capture moments and light as they came and left.

But the other feeling turned his stomach like a capsized boat.

It wasn't the guilt he had over suggesting that Hype should come along. There was guilt there, to be sure, but Calef recognized it and was dealing with it to the best of his abilities. No, his problem was that he couldn't explain who or what had attacked them. He tried to logically lay it out, but kept coming up short. There was no animal he knew of that he could identify as the beast in a confident way. It was otherworldly.

In other words, he found himself having to believe in something unbelievable.

And the way his dad looked at him in the morning meant he knew it, too.

10

"No time like the present," Joe said.

"Ain't that right," the Loner agreed. "Let's get the hell out of here."

One by one, the site team drove out of the cave on their hovermobiles and followed the Loner through the rest of the canyon. By grace alone, the rest of the journey out was uneventful.

The walls ended. They were now in a clearing that took their collective, chilly breaths away: the asteroid impact field.

It stretched on for kilometers, farther than anyone could see with their plain eyes. The asteroid had absolutely destroyed the town of Toowoomba, like a planet had decided to lay down and make a snow angel.

Rebecca stared at the arctic desert in awe. Alva, Maya, Joan and Calef did the same. The rest of the Knights, however, wasted no time once they arrived, taking off just seconds later.

"What's their hurry?" the Loner asked.

"I don't know," Rebecca said, "but I have a feeling we should find out."

Joe and Will had maps displayed that none of the other team members had access to. The two of them were in the lead, with Jan close behind, and Abe and Isaac another hundred meters back.

Since Alva was driving the hovermobile that Rebecca was riding on, she was looking for a digiscope in her supply bag. There wasn't one packed. Alva's bag was missing one, too. Thankfully, the Loner had one and lent it to Rebecca.

Rebecca looked through it. Digiscopes allowed the viewer to see far distances, and it also scanned the surroundings and collected data. She zoomed in on the Knights. They were clearly on a mission.

"Something feels off," she said. The Knights were heading for a patch of small rocks in the distance.

"What do you mean?" Alva asked.

"I don't know," she said, and felt stupid for not being able to put her finger on it. She zoomed some more. Then she felt the pulse. "The rocks don't look right."

"What does that mean, 'the rocks don't look right'?" Calef asked.

"There's a group of rocks out there, and a few of them don't look like the other rocks," she said. "Loner, can I take still images with this digiscope?"

"Sure," the Loner said.

Rebecca snapped some photos and sent them to her comm back on the Sea Eagle. Then she looked back in the digiscope. They had arrived at the rocks, but she couldn't make out what they were doing.

Joe and Will almost leapt off their hovermobiles. Joe pressed a button under his steering system and the back of his hovermobile opened, revealing a large storage space. Joe and Will picked up one of the strange rocks and dropped it in the space. And then another. And another. Until all four of the wrong-looking rocks were secured in his vehicle.

"That was efficient," Jan said with an uneasy smile as she pulled up. "You just knew you wanted those rocks, then?"

"Yes," Will said. "Please feel free to choose your own samples and conduct as thorough of a survey as you can. We are the first people of Flora to visit this site, so the more personal data we can collect, the better. We can learn much here."

Jan nodded with suspicion, and looked from Will to Joe. Joe's eyes darted down to the ground like he had noticed some personal data to collect, but all Jan saw was the ground.

The team did as they were instructed. They spread out in pairs, gathering what they could carry, learning what there was to be taught.

Abe and Isaac were in charge of collecting and testing the soil in different areas. Jan was observing as much as she could, and taking measurements of air quality and radioactivity. Will and Joe had already done the first thing they came to do.

Rebecca and Alva were allowed to do their own surveying.

"Hey," Alva said.

"Hey, yourself," Rebecca said.

"I like you," he said.

"Cool story, bro," she said. His face turned a burning red, contrasting his cool blue top. She laughed hysterically.

"That's not funny," he said.

"Yeah, it is," she said, "and you know it. Now, do you actually like me or do you just like me because you thought I was going to die?"

"I like you and now I find it imperative to tell you because I thought you were going to die."

"That is a very good answer," she said.

"I wonder if she's being as nice to him as you are to me," he said, pointing to their friends.

Calef had been brought on as a guide, so there was no task here for him. Maya kept him company as he played fetch with his dog in the crater of a great asteroid.

It's hard to describe the smell of cold. The smell is more of a feeling. Crisp is not a smell. Biting is not a smell. Nor is piercing or sharp. They're all things you feel that lend themselves to how a cold world smells.

Without a true smell, you would think that nostalgia would be harder to come by in an icy climate. But that isn't right at all. Calef was, in this moment, traveling from now to countless different points through his life in his mind, transported by the chill. He was here and he was not.

"Are you okay?" Maya asked.

"Yeah," Calef said. "I was just somewhere else. Sometime else."

She was sitting close to him. Her smell was sweet, the smell of warmth. That smell threw Calef in a different direction through time. Joan jumped on his lap. Her breath was a different kind of warm smell. Another direction, another memory.

The cold and the smells all brought him back to his mother.

"I'm sorry about that thing I said last night, about our kids," he said. "I was going through a lot at the moment."

"I hear you," she said. "I was going through a lot, too. There was this crazy beast in a cave."

"Right," he said, picking up the ball of tape he was throwing for Joan's sake.

"Let's take it one step at a time, then," she said.

"What do you mean?" he asked.

"A date," she said. "We can't do a whole ass life together without taking that first step."

"Are you asking me out?" he said.

"I am not," she said. "I merely said that we would have to go on a date before we go have a couple of kids together."

"Would you go on a date with me?" he asked.

She sat there in silence. She was looking past him.

"Are you really going to play me like that?" he asked. "You're just going to —"

"Shut up," she said. Her finger slowly pointed over his shoulder.

In the distance, a dozen Neo Atheists on hovermobiles were heading their way.

11

"Shit."

Calef took a moment to assess their arrival. He called to Joan, who hopped on the back of his hovermobile and took shelter under the tarp.

"We gotta go," he told Maya. She got on her vehicle and they took off towards the rest of the group. Calef opened a line to everyone.

"We have a group of Neo Atheists incoming from the east," he said. "We're heading back in your direction."

"Are you fucking kidding me?" Alva's voice exploded from their earpieces.

"Everyone, check your maps," Jan said. "Meet up with Will and Joe on the grid."

"Do not do that," Will said abruptly.

"What he means is, Abe and Isaac are in a more centralized location to the rest of you," Joe said, not covering for Will like he thought he was. "Meet at their point."

The team did as Joe instructed. Soon, they all met at the grid point, facing each other in a circle like spokes on a wheel.

"What now?" Alva asked.

"We take them head on," Will said.

"Go for it, cowboy," Calef said. "We're outpersonned and outgunned."

"Can we run for it?" Isaac asked.

"We can try," Calef said. "It might be our best chance. But they know this area better than any of us."

"Well, if those are our two options," Alva said, "then we're fucked."

Joe showed Will something on his comm.

"We're standing our ground," Will said. "Trust me."

"We do," Abe said.

"No," Calef said, starting his hovermobile back up. "Come on, dad."

"Son," Abe said. "I trust Will." Isaac looked torn between them.

Calef couldn't leave his family. Frustrated, he slammed on his steering wheel and turned off his hovermobile.

The Neo Atheists approached. They slowed down, now wary as to why the Knights weren't running. They stopped about twenty meters away.

These Neo Atheists all wore helmets, like the Knights did, but theirs were decorated in a more personal fashion, adorned with natural elements; one of the helmets had massive elk horns protruding from the sides, another the tail of a beaver flapping out the back. The Neo Atheist in front opened the visor of his helmet, revealing the face of the Cosmic Kangaroo.

"Do you believe in God, the Planner, the Plan?" he asked.

"You're damn right we do," Will said with pride.

"What is wrong with you?" Alva asked. Several members of the team sighed, exasperated.

"Thank you for your honesty," the marsupial-man said. The entire group of Neo Atheists raised their laserguns and pointed them at the Knights.

Then the Cosmic Kangaroo exploded into itty bits.

Everyone jumped back on both sides. Will started laughing maniacally.

"You dare challenge God?" he said. "He is all. He sees all. He hears all. He created all. He can destroy all. And He is on our side."

Blasts started raining down on the Neo Atheists. Calef looked up; the Sea Eagle was directly above them, Talons fixed and operational once more. Joe had shown Will a message from the ship; they knew the Sea Eagle would be arriving in moments.

Another Neo Atheist splattered into red nothing. The Atheists hurriedly restarted their hovermobiles to turn around and retreat; however, the Sea Eagle was unrelenting in its revenge. Calef couldn't count any survivors as the elevator lowered to bring them all back in.

"That is the power of God, my son," Abe said to Calef, smiling.

"It's funny you say that," Calef said. "Because when I looked around, God was nowhere to be found."

. . .

The team was happy to be back in the air.

They took off all their gear and were told by Joe to meet in the Chest in a half hour to debrief. Rebecca seemed off to Calef.

"Hey, you okay?" he asked.

"I don't know," she said. "I'm going back to my room to check on something. Can we talk before this debriefing?"

"Of course," he said.

This gave him a chance to say a few words to his father.

He tracked down Abe in his cabin. He felt it again, as he confronted his father.

The world dimming.

The lights on them growing.

Intermission was over.

Act II

CALEF walks up to his father angrily, with
purpose.

CALEF: Why do you do that?

ABE: Why do I do what?

CALEF: Why do you let people hate behind
the guise of faith?

ABE: I don't know what you mean.

CALEF: He called me *boy*. He called me *son*.

ABE: Those are just words.

CALEF: We all know what those words mean
and why he chooses to use them.

ABE: He does not have hate in his heart.

CALEF: I don't trust him.

ABE: You don't have to.

CALEF: Why do you? Why do you trust him
so completely?

ABE: I don't. But I trust the Lord. And he is a man of the Lord.

CALEF: He is a man of himself. You chose him over me just now.

ABE: And he was right. What is the point of this conversation, Calef? We've had this one so many times. You think we're a bunch of hypocrites. Big whoop. All humans are hypocritical. No one can hold up to even their own standards, much less God's.

CALEF: So we stop trying? What I don't get is you keep acting like we live in this post-racial world. That world doesn't exist! As long as people have eyes and self-interest and seek power over others, we will always live in a racist world. But your faith claims to be able to fix that. That we should be able to see each other as sisters and brothers, that there is no color, that we are all just equal children before God. And your faith has tried that for thousands of years and things for us have barely moved a centimeter.

ABE: You use the metric system now?

CALEF: The whole universe uses it but you stubborn assholes.

ABE: We can be stuck in our ways.

CALEF: And that gets in humanity's way.

ABE: You say this because you don't trust one Christian?

CALEF: I say this because I don't trust religion.

ABE: You don't mean that.

CALEF: I do. Religion kills.

ABE: It saves.

CALEF: It kills people while telling them they'll be saved. All religions have a history of persecution. I'm tired of talking about the big ways. Like the fact that the Nazis used passages of the Bible to justify the genocide of the Jewish people, because they were responsible for the murder of Jesus. I could name giant historical examples all day. No, I want to talk about the small ways.

ABE: Then talk.

CALEF: The micro-aggressions. The things people say that you brush off because you both believe in the same thing. Or both *claim* to believe in the same thing. But belief and practice are two different animals, too. When someone says he's not a racist because he believes in Jesus, but he says and does racist things, do his beliefs mean any damn thing at all?

ABE: That's enough.

CALEF: This isn't a rhetorical conversation. When I was a Neo Atheist, I was forced to look at the world every day and decide whether religion was objectively making the world a better place or a worse one. Do you know what the world said when I asked which it was? "No comment."

ABE: I don't understand you. Maybe I should talk in a language you understand. Do you think you're the hero? Do you think you're Luke Skywalker from those old movies you loved as a kid?

CALEF: I'm not a hero and I don't pretend to be.

ABE: What do you think this is? You're on the hero's journey right now!

CALEF: This is not the hero's journey. I'm not going into the dark forest. I know all of these places already. I'm dealing with who I am now and who I used to be.

ABE: And with God's help, you can be a beacon.

CALEF: I ain't no beacon.

ABE: Son, if you don't want to believe in anything, that's up to you. It breaks my heart, but you are your own man. But for you to tell me my beliefs make me worse . . . that just makes me think you don't know me at all.

CALEF: I'm not saying you're worse. I'm just asking, do you really think you're much better?

ABE: I do. And I wish you believed in something that made you feel the way God allows me to.

CALEF: But I do.

ABE: And what is that?

An audience member stepped onto the stage. It was Rebecca, Joan by her side.

"I'm sorry to interrupt," she said. "But Calef, we need to talk. Immediately."

Calef took a look at his father.

"We will finish this later," Abe said.

"Maybe it is finished," Calef said, and left the cabin with Rebecca. She was walking fast.

"Slow down," Calef said. "What's going on?"

"We can't talk until we get back to my room," she said. They walked past the dining area. Both Alva and Maya were in there, and noticed them pass. They looked at each other and followed behind.

Rebecca was almost running now.

"Stop!" Calef said, grabbing Rebecca's hand. "What the hell is going on?" Joan barked. Alva and Maya caught up to them, and they all stood in a hallway. Rebecca took a deep breath, and her voice shook when she spoke.

"I think I found proof that the Christians killed the world."

12

"Which time?" Calef asked.

Rebecca let out a high-pitched, unexpected laugh; the pressure building inside her upon her revelation found a valve for escape. She led Calef, Alva, Maya and Joan into her cabin and shut the door behind them.

"Remember how I said the rocks didn't look right?" she started.

"Yeah," Calef said. "I'm still not sure what that means."

"I had the foresight to take some still images with the Loner's digiscope and had them sent back to my comm here," she said. "Take a look at this."

She displayed an image on a tablet for them all to see. The rocks in the picture didn't look to be natural at all. The edges were too smooth. They looked like they had been designed by man. And that was when Calef saw it.

"Are those serial numbers?" he asked.

"They are," she said. She took a deep breath. "This goes into a conspiracy theory that I never thought had a drop of truth to it, but here we are. Here I am, questioning everything."

"So what is the theory in question?" Alva asked.

"There has been a rumor since it happened that the asteroid was driven here, by people. There isn't a lot of evidence, or wasn't any, to back it up, but there are some odd threads. For a while, it looked like the asteroid's trajectory was shifting, and it was going to miss us altogether. Something put it back on course, and most of us assumed that was just the random nature of the universe. But the theory is it was propelled."

"Rockets?" Calef asked.

"That's what these look like," Rebecca said. She pulled up more images, and sure enough, the four not-rocks appeared to have exhaust systems underneath. Some of them had a sharp tooth or two hanging off; those could have potentially been part of a claw used to latch onto the asteroid.

"You're saying you think someone did this on purpose," Maya said. She did not sound naïve. She sounded disappointed. "Is there a prime suspect?"

"It was clearly the fucking Knights," Alva said.

"Why?" Maya asked.

"The better question might be *to what end?*" Calef said. "We know the Knights funded the tech and travel to Flora. They built the initial settlements. Over 90% of the planet is Christian, and many of those people converted after leaving Earth. This isn't coincidental. It's causational."

"The Knights made this planet cold to make more people believe what they believe," Rebecca concluded.

"Why does everybody suck?" Alva asked. "Why can't people just let other people be? They fucked up a whole planet on behalf of their bullshit."

"I'm sorry," Maya said, seemingly apologizing for her entire population.

"You didn't do this," Calef said. "You have your own thing, too. I believe that. And I don't think you knew about this, either."

"I didn't, Calef," she said. "I swear. And I don't think most of the people on this ship or on my planet do, either."

"We know two people who do," Rebecca said. "Will and Joe. If Joe doesn't know everything, he knows enough to be Will's right-hand man."

"Yeah, for jerking him off," Alva said, still disgusted.

"What do we do?" Maya asked. "Do we confront him?"

"No," Calef said. "We keep this quiet, and we keep going. If this is a cover-up for a big lie, then I have a feeling the 'phoenix' we're looking for is anything but. We stay quiet, lay low, and keep our enemies close. All that jazz."

Rebecca and Alva nodded in agreement. Joan barked, solemnly promising to keep her adorable muzzle shut. Maya was the only one who looked uncertain.

"I'm not asking you to lie, Maya," Calef said.

"Just omit the truth I can't forget," she said.

"Just for the time being," he said. Maya nodded.

Will, who had been standing outside their cabin for long enough to hear the majority of the conversation, knocked on the door.

"Who is it?" Rebecca asked.

"It's Will," he said. "It's time for the debriefing. Bring all of your friends."

They looked at each other and said not one more word. They waited a moment, and then made their way back to the Chest.

. . .

"Reed Harper – Hype – was one of the kindest men I have ever met."

So started Joe on his eulogy for Hype.

"I first met him when he was just a teenager. It was at a bible camp. His enthusiasm for the Word and the Lord was infectious, as was his love for life. He was secretly dating a girl from the camp across the lake, which wasn't really a secret to anybody. That girl, Rachel, would eventually become his wife."

Joe had to pause. He looked to be trying to place another thought in his mind to alleviate the feelings he was having.

"They never had any children. Not yet. It was in their future. A future that, for Hype – for Reed – instead ended on this cold excuse of a planet."

The crew nodded enthusiastically in agreement. It wasn't always there, but in this moment, Calef could physically feel the disdain the people of Flora had for Earth. It was inexplicable, irrational, to despise people for no reason at all. Except the people of Flora felt like they *did* have their reasons. The death of one of their own was just more ineffable proof that they were good, and Earth was bad.

"We will not let his death be in vain," Joe said. There was hollering in approval. "We will complete this mission. We will raise the phoenix, and we will bring warmth, prosperity and faith back to this forsaken place. Amen."

"Amen," the crew said.

Joe, now joined by Will, told the story of their journey to the rest of the ship. They elaborated, of course, but all the main plot points were there. The Neo Atheists. The mammoths. The leviathan. Then they talked about collecting samples and the massive amount of data they had sent back to Flora.

But they never mentioned the not-rocks.

The crew was dismissed. Will stopped Calef.

"You mind if I talk to you for a moment?" Will asked.

"Sure," Calef said. They walked over to a dining area. Calef picked up a cup of coffee and Will eyed some donuts. "What's up?"

"I let the Loner stay," Will said. "Gave her a cabin. I figured it was the least we could do, give her a ride back to America for saving our lives."

"That sounds right to me," Calef said.

"Good, good," Will said. "Glad we're on the same page. Say, we turned in all of the data we collected. Did your friend Rebecca get anything good while we out there that she might want to share with the rest of the class?"

Will knowingly smiled. He put his hand on Calef's shoulder.

"Oddly enough, all of our digiscopes were missing from our bags," Calef said. "So we were as disappointed as anyone would be that we were not able to participate."

Check. Will didn't anticipate his own sabotage being turned on him.

"That's a shame," Will said. "For sure. Well, if she did get anything, just be sure to turn it in."

"Will do," Calef said, toasting Will with his cup of steaming coffee as he walked away.

"Smooth," Maya said. She had been watching them from a table close by.

"Right?" Calef said. "It just came to me."

"So all you Earthers *are* just a bunch of liars," she said, shaking her head. "Just like my mama told me."

"At least I never tried to destroy your planet," he said. "Until today, I just thought those were nasty rumors."

. . .

Abe knocked on Isaac's door.

"Son," Abe said. "Can I talk to you?"

Isaac wasn't sure how to respond. He silently nodded.

"I am very grateful we made it through that alive," Abe said. "As much as your mother is calling to me."

"Me, too," Isaac said.

"I wanted to tell you that I'm just grateful that you are alive," Abe said.

Isaac again had no response.

"Sometimes my head gets so full of thoughts that I forget how to love," Abe said. "And I love you. I do. Not the person I think you should be. I love the person that you are. I love your soul, son."

Megan was watching them from across the hall in her cabin. Tears threatened to escape her eyes and she quickly cleared them with the inside of her hands. Isaac embraced his father, and Abe held on tight to his son. Megan walked over and threw her arms around both of them.

Will's voice filled the ship over the intercom.

"Our ETA back to America is less than two hours. In that time, I suggest you get your rest, as the chances are probable that, once we land in the Great Lakes area, we will encounter the Neo Atheists yet again. We will need focus, we will need strength, and we will have the Lord on our side, as always. Amen."

Amen could be heard echoing down the empty hallways.

13

"I'm gonna kick your ass," the Loner said.

"We'll see," Calef smiled. They were in a training room on the Sea Eagle. Both were wearing virtual reality headsets and vests that could recreate physical sensations in real life.

Like getting shot with lasers.

They were in a jungle recreated by pixels. The training room itself had its heat raised and was filled with a foggy mist. Calef was examining his surroundings. He saw a monkey up in a tree. The monkey quickly looked behind itself, to the east. Calef knew where the Loner was hiding.

He snuck from tree to tree, knowing his opponent could be around the next one. After a dozen or so trees, however, she was nowhere to be found.

Zap!

Zap!

Two blasts past the back of his head, into the tree. Calef slowly turned around, his hands up in the air.

"How did you get behind me?" he asked.

"I saw that damn monkey looking at me," she said, and held up said monkey by the tail. "I shot that son of a bitch and then did a big circle around."

"Well done," he said. "But you don't know where my teammate is."

"I don't," she said. She tossed the dead monkey into a bush, her lasergun still pointed at him. "But mine is out there, too."

. . .

The Loner's teammate, Alva, was trying to be the monkey himself. He was up in a tree, scanning as far and wide as he could see for Rebecca, Calef's teammate. He spotted a vine and gripped it, swinging from one tree to the next.

He knew she was messing with him. There was no way he was at an advantage against her, and that had been true since the day they met. She was the kind of person that always made him want to be better.

He grabbed onto another vine and began another swing. Halfway through, he felt his lower back vibrate from laser shots fired down below. The vine was cut by a blast and he fell to the jungle floor on his back.

"I give!" he said. "Please have mercy on me."

He looked up and the person who shot him wasn't Rebecca at all.

. . .

Calef and the Loner circled one another. He was trying to figure out her game. Why was she holding him hostage and not just finishing him off right now?

Before he could formulate an answer, blasts came out of the bushes to his right. They struck the Loner again and again.

"Damn!" the Loner cursed, as Rebecca revealed herself from the jungle. Seconds later, Alva burst from the other side of the clearing.

Zap!

Rebecca shot Alva, too.

"Shoot," Alva said. "We done?"

"Sure," Rebecca said, her eyebrow raised. "We should get ready for landing."

. . .

The four of them picked up Joan from Megan's room and walked together to the Chest. Will and Joe were chatting next to a station when they arrived.

"Just the person I wanted to see," Will said.

"What's up, Will?" Calef said.

"Not you," Will said. He pointed at the Loner. "Her. You said you're from the Great Lakes area, right?"

"I am," she said.

"Okay," he continued. "Our destination is Isle Royale National Park."

"I know it well," she said. Then she looked confused. "It used to be an island on Lake Superior before all the lakes froze over."

"We can't land the Sea Eagle on the lake, regardless of the ice," he said. "We need a good, solid site to put her down on, and then we'll take a small team on hovermobiles to Isle Royale like we did in Australia."

"Because that went really well?" Calef said.

"Because we have to," Will finished.

"We should land in Grand Portage," the Loner said. "That's where I'm from, and it's probably the closest we can land without crossing into Neo Atheist territory. They run most of the Canadian border."

"Then those are our coordinates," Will said to Joe. "Set those and let me notify the team."

"Who's on the team?" Calef asked.

"It's got to be small," Will said.

"Who?" Calef asked again.

"Me," Will said. "You. Rebecca. Joe. Jeff. Abe. The Loner. Everyone else stays behind. Including that dog of yours."

"Bullshit," Calef said. "Don't I have a say in this?" Leaving behind Joan and Alva and Maya and bringing along someone named Jeff, a man he didn't even know, all felt wrong.

"You don't," Will said. "This is the most important mission the planet of Flora has ever assigned, and I have sole discretion over its execution."

"Alva?" Rebecca said. "Don't you have anything to say?"

"No," Alva said, his eyes staring at the floor. "I don't know what I'm doing out there and if he doesn't think I should go, then maybe I shouldn't."

Alarms went off in Rebecca's head.

"Okay," Calef said. "Fine."

The entire team looked at Calef like he had stripped off his clothes without warning. *Stay quiet, lay low, keep our enemies close*, he had told everybody else. He had to follow his own plan.

"Let's get ready then, right?" Calef said, clapping his hands together, nodding to Joan, Rebecca, Alva and the Loner to follow him back to their cabins.

Once they were out of earshot, Rebecca asked Alva what the hell was going on. Alva spoke barely a decibel over a whisper.

"In the VR game, Will was there. In the jungle. He shot me, and then he threatened to hurt you and Joan if I didn't stay behind."

"That motherfucker threatened my dog?!" Calef said.

"Yeah," Alva said, "and I believe him when he says he'll do it."

"What is going on?" the Loner asked. "What did I miss?"

"That's why I brought you back here with us," Calef said. "We have to catch you up."

They explained to the Loner everything that they discovered at the asteroid site. Funnily enough, the Loner barely reacted. She seemed to have the same kind of general disdain for the Florans as they did for Earthers. She was not surprised that they were capable of such shenanigans.

Rebecca asked to be excused for a moment. She left the room, and Alva followed her. The Loner silently speculated over what the phoenix could be for a minute and then Rebecca and Alva were back in the cabin.

With everyone on the same page, they headed back to the Chest. Calef, Rebecca and the Loner met up with the rest of the phoenix team, who were standing in the middle of the room: Will, Abe, Joe and Jeff. Jeff was the biggest man on the ship, with no hair on his head and all of it hanging over his lip in a massive red mustache. He said nothing when the rest of them joined their circle, instead just crossing his python arms.

"The hovermobiles are all ready," Joe said. "Our mechanics looked them over and made sure they were good as new after the last trip." He nodded too much, in a way that rang false and tipped them off to remain vigilant with their vehicles.

The phoenix team walked to the elevator and were lowered into the garage. They all returned to the hovermobiles they had used before. Jeff walked over to a dark corner of the level to the biggest vehicle in their arsenal; it had been wrapped under a tarp earlier, so nobody had even seen it. It appeared to have been some kind of heavy-duty jeep before it was retrofitted with hover tech. It was carrying boxes strapped down to its bed.

"Christmas presents?" Calef asked.

"We need a way to wake the phoenix," Will said. "Those will do the job."

"Dad, do you know what's in those boxes?" Calef asked Abe.

"Oh, yes, my son," Abe said with an easy smile. "Those are bombs."

14

Calef was definitely not comfortable with his father's level of comfort.

"Were you going to mention we've been carrying bombs on this ship the entire time?" he asked.

"Why?" Abe said. "It wouldn't have changed anything if I had."

"I probably wouldn't have had Joe over there spinning the ship round and round while we shot at the bad guys who were also shooting at us," Calef said.

"And then we would have probably died," Abe said. "It was better you didn't know."

"How does he actually have a point here?" Rebecca asked.

"Abe might be the smartest one of us all," Will said. Abe smiled and nodded and Calef seethed at what he considered condescension. Then Calef wondered how he could possibly be mad that somebody called his dad smart and he decided to check his bias, no matter how well-met.

The team started their engines, and the elevator continued their journey down to the ground. Unlike Australia, the weather here was not kind. It was snowing hard, and almost horizontally. The crew had their helmets on and were generally warm under all their equipment, but the temperature was several degrees below freezing with the wind-chill.

There were four retractable pillars holding the Sea Eagle up, so it was landed securely on the surface, which allowed it to self-diagnose and recharge. The weight of the ship was likely enough to push those pillars through the ice if they would have parked on Lake Superior.

Instead, they were sitting on the west side of Grand Portage, a tiny town where the Loner used to live. They started heading east through the village and towards Isle Royale. The Loner began giving the team an impromptu tour of her home, using the helmet comms to speak to them all.

"That was the school where Molly worked. She turned that building across the street into a mosque, but she let all kinda folks do whatever religion they wanted there." They heard her gulp. "We had such a tight community."

"What happened?" Rebecca asked.

"There had been an agreement," the Loner said. "With the Neo Atheists. They don't usually make pacts, but there was as many of us as there was of them so it made sense for them. There's a line between our town and their territory. The only rule was to stay on our side of the line."

"If this is too much . . ." Rebecca started.

"No," the Loner said. "You're my friends now. You should know. Molly was so bothered by the line.

She couldn't understand why we couldn't be kind to our neighbors. I tried to explain to her again and again that our neighbors didn't understand kindness. They didn't want to be friends. But Molly saw how scared the kids were. How scared the adults were. She wanted peace."

The Loner took a breath.

"So one day she walked up to the line. She called for them. She said . . ."

The Loner's voice broke.

"She said that she wanted to be neighbors. Real neighbors. The kind who look out for each other. The kind who lend each other a hand if the other needs help. The kind who can make this world a better place together. A Neo Atheist showed up while she was hollering. He said his name was Darius. Molly got closer. She thought . . ."

Another pause.

"She thought that she was about to make a difference. Change the world. She took one step over the line, and Darius asked —"

"Do you believe in God, the Plan, the Planner?" Calef finished.

"Yeah," the Loner said. "She said, 'With all my heart.' Then he shot her in hers."

The comm was quiet for a moment as they continued through town.

"I'm sorry," Rebecca said.

"That was our house right there," the Loner said, pointing to a small cottage ahead. "Wait a second – those sons of bitches!"

They all noticed that one of the windows was broken.

"I'm sorry, but I have to stop here," she said.

"Absolutely not," Will said. "We have to continue on."

"Then go on without me," she said.

"Nope," Calef said. "We're friends now."

And the Loner and her friends went to investigate.

. . .

Alva and Joan were snuggling in his cot. She put her snout under his chin and whined.

"I know," he said. "This sucks."

"Hey," a voice from across the room said. Alva looked up to see Megan and Isaac standing in his doorway.

"Hey," he said. "You're Calef's brother and sister, right?"

"Right," said Isaac.

"We have a weird question for you," Megan said.

"Shoot," Alva said.

"Would you tell us what our brother is like?" Isaac asked. Alva wasn't sure what they meant.

"We've missed almost 14 years of each other's lives," Megan said. "And you got to be there for it all. We just want to know our brother."

"Yeah," Alva said. "I can do that. As long as you tell me the embarrassing shit he did as a kid."

"Deal," Megan said.

"Is it okay if I sit in, too?" another voice from beyond the doorway asked. Maya stepped into view.

"Yeah, I think you better get in on this, too," Alva said. Joan shook her head at the disloyalty of these humans.

. . .

The Loner crept up and looked into the broken window.

"You've got to be kidding me," she said. She walked slowly over to the door, which was unlocked. She swung it open, and they all saw her quaint living room, except it had been completely torn apart and it wasn't a question by whom.

"Why?" she asked. "Haven't they done enough?"

"They're animals," Will said. "You can't expect them to act civilized."

"Oh, you should talk," she said. Calef and Rebecca's eyes got wide. "Like y'all are any better."

"What is that supposed to mean?" Will asked. He shot looks at every person in the room.

"You know what I mean," she said. "Hypocrites. Each and every one of you. Jesus told y'all what to do thousands of years ago and your mouths flap that you understand, but your actions say you are *all* animals. Selfish, cruel animals. Don't care about nobody but yourselves and what *you* believe. Hell, animals know better to know what facts are and what stories are."

The Loner looked back to the ruins of what her life used to be.

"Molly didn't deserve this. She didn't deserve to be hurt by animals. She deserved to be loved. She deserved to live a long, good life. Nobody saved her. Nobody stepped in to stop that man from killing the woman I loved. Including me. We all failed Molly. Maybe I failed her the most."

The Loner fell to her knees. She could feel small pieces of glass digging into her leg. She could still smell cinnamon apple candle wax. Maybe if she found one of the candles and lit its wick, she could bring Molly back.

"It's time to go," Will said.

"Jesus, man," Calef said.

"Keep that name out of your mouth, boy," Will said.

"Do *not* speak to my son like that," Abe said, stepping between the two of them.

Will said nothing. He turned around and left the cottage, Jeff and Joe close behind.

"Good luck with the Neo Atheists," Calef shouted behind them.

"It did Hype a lot of good to have you along with us, wouldn't you say?" Will said. Calef lunged at him. He drove him back across the front porch and slammed him down on the ground.

"Calef!" Abe said.

"This is just who you are," Will said, as calm as he'd ever been. "People don't change their stripes. You stayed here on this cold world because it is what you deserve and you know it."

Calef squeezed his grip on Will's collar for another moment before letting go and standing up. He walked away and back onto his hovermobile. Rebecca and the Loner followed suit.

Without another word, the phoenix team rode away from the cottage and back towards Isle Royale. They had no idea that they were being watched by Neo Atheists the entire time.

15

"That is hilarious," Alva said. The whole room was laughing. "How did Calef not know there was bird shit in his hair?"

"No idea," Megan said. "By the time he noticed, it was well frozen in there."

There was a knock at the cabin door. Alva answered it. There was a group of men that he hadn't met yet waiting outside.

"Sorry to interrupt. My name is Philip. For your safety, we're going to need you all to come with us," the man in front said.

"For our safety?" Alva said. "What the fuck are you talking about?"

"It's just a precaution," Philip said.

"A precaution against what?" Alva asked. Philip stayed silent. "You're locking us up."

Alva shoved Philip into the rest of his group.

"Run!" he said, but they hadn't a chance to from the start. Philip stood right back up and grabbed Alva by the shoulders. Joan started barking, and then tried to jump on Philip. Philip swung his arm back and hit Joan, sending her to the ground. Maya screamed.

"Look," Philip said, "we can do this the hard way, but I would prefer we all just walk to the safe room together."

"What are you claiming to be protecting us from?" Maya asked.

"Yourselves," Philip said. Isaac and Megan looked at each other, and then Maya. They nodded and all of them peacefully left the cabin of their own accord. Alva had his hands brought behind his back and held there by Philip. Joan flinched.

"It's okay," Maya said, her thumb brushing Joan's face. "Let's go."

They were led to the safe room, surrounded by the Knights.

. . .

The phoenix team had resumed their speed but were more fractured than ever. They would be arriving at Isle Royale soon and, hopefully, Calef thought, this would all be over.

"Can you hear me?" a voice asked in Calef's ear. It was the Loner. "This is a direct line from me to you."

"Yeah, I hear you," he said. "What's up?"

"We're being followed," she said. "Neo Atheists. I can feel it."

"Why are you telling me privately?" he asked.

"Because I'm giving you a choice," she said. "I'm letting you decide whether we should tell them all, or lead him into it." She nodded over to Will.

Calef shouldn't have hesitated. But he did. He thought about it. He considered that the world might actually be a better a place without people like Will in it.

And then he remembered that it wasn't his choice to make.

"They're here," Calef said, opening a channel to entire team. "Neo Atheists. They're on our tail."

Everyone started looking around frantically, and while Calef realized his mistake in the way he revealed this information to the team, the Neo Atheists realized that the Knights knew they were there.

Pew!

Pew!

Pew!

Laser blasts from the left and right. The phoenix team was speeding along on a relatively open space, but it was lined by woods on each side. The Neo Atheists had been hiding amongst those trees, riding close by but out of sight. The element of surprise removed, they had to refer to their violence.

The phoenix team drew their laserguns, returning fire to an invisible enemy while trying to drive away from it. It wasn't slowing the Neo Atheists' attack. It certainly wasn't stopping it.

"We have to drive closer to the trees," Calef said.

"That's suicide," Will said.

"No, staying in the middle is," Calef said. "We're fish in an ice hole. If we can't see them, we can't shoot them. We have to split and take a side."

"Will, you and Jeff follow me," the Loner said. "The rest trail Calef."

Calef looked over to the Loner. She blew him a kiss. Then she led Will and Jeff to the left towards their tree line. Calef led his side – Rebecca, Abe and Joe – to the right.

The Loner had no fear, not of the Neo Atheists, and certainly not of death. Will assumed she was going to stop at the edge of the woods, but instead she drove right into them, surprising the Neo Atheists maneuvering through the trees. She rammed right into one, quickly pulling away as it exploded into the trunk of a tall pine. She pulled back out of the woods and in front once more.

"Nice work," Jeff said, impressed by her guts. Not to be outdone, he took a turn inside the forest. He pulled up behind two Neo Atheists driving side-by-side. He shot them both in the back of the head, hitting them in the space between their helmets and their jackets, killing them both instantly. Their limp bodies fell back off their hovermobiles, which then swerved off in opposite directions before being stopped in their tracks by other trees. Jeff let out a laugh.

The Loner thought he'd return like she had, but Jeff had had a taste and was thirsty now. He knew there were none behind him, because there were no laser blasts coming from that direction, and he could see four weaving their way through the woods in front of him. He was determined to end them all.

On the other side, Calef was having much more trouble. Joe was the only other person trained in any kind of combat, so he and Calef were the sole members of their group who were capable of taking anybody out. Abe and Rebecca understood that they were just firing to cover themselves at this point; there was no real attempt to end any lives.

"I'm going in there," Joe said.

"I'm coming," Calef said.

"You have to stay out here and defend them," Joe said, referring to the rest of their party. "I've got this."

Joe drove his hovermobile into the woods. He immediately ran into one of the Neo Atheists, who he hadn't seen before he made his way in. They collided, and Joe flew off the side of his hovermobile, holding on with just one hand. The Neo Atheist fired at him several times and missed, giving Joe an opportunity to get back in his seat and ram the Neo Atheist again. The Atheist changed the target of his lasergun to Joe's hovermobile itself; after a few more pulls of the trigger, Joe's hovermobile exploded.

"Joe!" Calef yelled.

A giant ball of smoke was running alongside the Neo Atheist and his vehicle. Calef could see the back of Joe's craft was dragging along the ground, but he couldn't see Joe. The Atheist kept close and repeatedly fired into the smoke, until Joe's hovermobile exploded again, this time in a massive ball of flames.

Calef was speechless.

The smoke cleared, and Calef shoved his fist in the air with joy. Joe had managed to jump off his craft and onto the Atheist's. He had the Atheist in a headlock. Calef drove into the woods and right up next to them. He put his lasergun directly into the side of the Neo Atheist and pulled the trigger three times. The Atheist slumped over, and Joe threw him off the vehicle. They both pulled out of the woods and back into the open.

The Atheists were having a hell of a time with Jeff. He wouldn't slow down and he wouldn't stop, zigging and zagging behind them, seemingly impossible to hit. Jeff could have fired back, but he appeared to be having *fun*.

On both sides, simultaneously, the Atheists appeared to receive a message on their comms. They all left the woods for the open space in the middle, ahead of where the phoenix team was now and collecting together in the space they had been riding. When the team looked to where they were gathering, they finally noticed that another team of Neo Atheists had formed between them while they had been distracted on the sides. Now the entire group of Neo Atheists – nearly 20 hovermobiles in all – were driving straight down the open space. The Atheist who was leading the pack removed his face visor.

It was Darius. He smiled.

The Loner couldn't be stopped. She sped ahead of the others, knowing that this could be her only time to get vengeance.

"Loner, don't!" Calef pleaded.

"My name is Josephine," she said, with a wink. "If we ever meet again, you can call me Josie. And this is what Molly deserves."

She pulled a second lasergun out of a compartment in her craft. She pressed a button to fix her speed and stood up on her hovermobile, no longer using her hands to steer. She was driving straight into the pack of Neo Atheists, both guns blazing blue.

"Cover her!" Joe said. Both groups from the phoenix team met back in the middle, and they were behind the Loner and the pack. The Atheists were trying to shoot the Loner off her perch, but only a few at the back had a shot at her without hitting their fellow Atheists, and those few had little time to shoot, as she swiftly took out Atheist after Atheist, hovermobile after hovermobile. It started as two, then six, and then it was double figures.

Darius realized the Loner was quickly giving the Knights the upper hand. He looked ahead and saw a fork in the road created by another patch of woods.

"We need to go right," Will said. "That's the way to Isle Royale."

Darius gave the Neo Atheists another command, and then put his visor back on. The remaining Atheists started leaning left.

"Leave them be!" Calef begged the Loner.

But she could not.

"Maybe I'll see you in another life," she said. "But if we did this one right, maybe not. See you around, Calef."

And with that, the Loner was gone, along with what remained of the pack of Neo Atheists.

16

The safe room felt anything but.

Alva, Joan and Maya were on the floor, up against the wall, while Megan and Isaac were sitting on the only two chairs in the tiny space. Philip and his men had given them exactly zero pieces of real information, and hadn't returned since locking them in the room.

They figured they were probably being listened to, so nobody really had anything important to say, or felt like they could confidently share it. They just shared the silence instead, occasionally punctuated by Joan's sighs or light whining. She was stressed out. She was hungry. They all were.

. . .

The rest of the trip to Isle Royale was relatively uneventful.

There were only six of them now. The Loner didn't return, and Calef had a feeling their time together, for now, was over. As a fellow wanderer, he understood the flow of the universe, and he felt that stream part in a meaningful way. He wished her the best.

Though the Neo Atheists were absent from the remaining kilometers, their path was not clear. Isle Royale had been a national park for hundreds of years, a welcome spot for hikers and outdoorspeople, but the freezing of the Earth did not make it more easily navigable. Their travel was slow and careful; their cargo explosive in a literal way.

A half-hour after they had parted ways with the Loner, they reached the heart of the Isle.

"Sound the beacon," Will said. Joe typed a command into his comm. A chirp rang through the woods. "Follow that signal."

They rode their hovermobiles towards the birdsong, which was coming from a large pine tree that looked unnatural. It looked so because it was so. It was manmade, and behind one of the pieces of artificial bark was a hole.

Will pulled off a small necklace from around his neck. There was a cross hanging from it; that cross of Jesus doubled as a key fob. He pushed the bottom of the cross into the hole, turned it, and the land around them started to shake.

In a clearing some meters away, the floor of the forest started to open up from one side, sliding from the far end underneath the side closer to them. Inside the threshold was a stairway, akin to a cellar, except these steps led deep into the ground.

"Let's go find a phoenix," Calef said, tongue firmly planted in cheek.

"This is where your journey ends," Will said. "I'm afraid I can't allow you or her to pass this point."

Rebecca pressed a button on her comm.

"Why's that?" Calef asked.

"This part is for believers only," Will said.

"So the Neo Atheists aren't the only ones who discriminate here," Calef said.

"How dare you compare me to them," Will said.

"How dare you act like them," Calef said. "Dad, say something."

Abe stood for a moment in silence.

"He's right, son," Abe said. "This is not a place for you."

Calef disagreed. He started to walk towards the stairs. Jeff grabbed him by the shoulder.

"Get your hands off me, man," Calef said.

"Afraid I can't do that, brother," Jeff said.

"I am not your brother," Calef said.

"That makes this easier then," Jeff said, and then struck Calef in the head so hard he dropped to the earth, unconscious. Rebecca screamed. Abe looked away. Jeff dragged Calef over to a tree and started to unravel some rope.

"You can make this easy on yourself or you can end up like him," Jeff said to Rebecca. "Either way, you both will be tied to this tree."

. . .

Alva's comm went off.

Before Rebecca left, she told him to keep it on, hidden, and that she would send a signal if anything went wrong. For Alva, it wasn't a matter of *if*, but *when*. And the time was now.

"We need to get their attention," Alva said quietly.

"Why?" Isaac said.

"I have to get out of here," Alva said, showing them his comm. "Something is wrong."

"I got this," Isaac said. "Be ready."

Isaac stuck his finger all down the back of his throat without hesitation. Just as fast, his breakfast came gushing out of his mouth.

"Someone is sick in here!" Maya shouted at the door. "We need a medic!"

Philip calmly opened the door, his hand around his nose and mouth. Joan leaped out as soon as he took his first step in and pushed him down on his back. There were only two other men outside with him, and they were so surprised by the flying dog that they didn't see Alva and Isaac coming with their elbows. Both were knocked out and collapsed to the floor. Alva turned right back around and punched Philip in the face, leaving him an unconscious puddle. They took the trio's laserguns and headed down the hall towards the Chest.

The Chest was buzzing with activity. Their connection with the phoenix team was unstable due to the weather, so they were only getting random bits of information and none of it was particularly helpful. They were on standby in case of emergency. A laser blast towards the ceiling got the crew's attention.

"I am a secular Earther and I have no problem taking you Jesus-loving freaks out if you try to stop me from helping my friends," Alva said. Most of the remaining crew were not soldiers; they were Jesus-loving freaks with little-to-no combat training. Many of them put their hands up in the air immediately; it didn't seem clear to most why the Earthers were so hostile in the first place.

"Can you get us down to the garage?" Maya asked Isaac. He nodded. Laserguns raised, they moved to the floor of the Chest and Isaac took over elevator controls.

"You have to stay here," Alva said to Joan, scratching her behind the ear. "Protect your brother and sister," he said, pointing at Isaac and Megan. He and Maya got onto the elevator platform. Isaac lowered them into the garage.

"Godspeed," Isaac said. Alva stuck his tongue out at him. "You know what I mean."

. . .

"Are you awake?"

Calef opened his eyes to the sound of Rebecca's voice. His head was beating like a broken heart. His chest came in deep and he slowly pushed air through his lips. He was centering himself, focusing on his breathing.

"I'm here," he said.

"You're doing that breathing thing," she said.

"I am," he said. "I need you to do it with me."

"We already decided that we were not going to do that," she said jokingly.

"Shut up," he said, laughing. "Feel the ropes."

As their deep breaths started to align, she could feel the ropes tighten and then loosen around them.

"I think they were counting on me to stay passed out," he said. "We can probably get enough room in here for you to slip out, and once you get out, I can get out."

So they continued to sit together and breathe.

. . .

Alva and Maya put on some gear and jumped on individual hovermobiles. The door beneath the garage was opened to the world below, but the elevator wouldn't respond to them on their level. They figured Isaac had probably been compromised by now and hoped he was okay.

"So we jump?" Maya asked.

"We jump," Alva said.

They revved their hovermobiles and drove them through the opening, falling like angels to the earth far below.

They landed like children in a pile of leaves, snow thrown every way. Maya used Alva's comm to pinpoint Calef and Rebecca's location and was leading the way. Barring any interference, they would be there soon.

Maya only hoped it would be soon enough.

. . .

"I think I can," Rebecca said.

Calef had asked if she thought she could get through the space they had created through their breathing. Now they would alternate. Calef would take big breaths in, puffing his chest and creating even more space, and Rebecca would empty herself of air, taking up as little as she could.

Calef got big. Rebecca tried to slip down but panicked, breathing in unexpectedly and getting her face caught under the ropes. She started to struggle, flailing and feeling claustrophobic.

"It's okay," Calef said. "I'm here with you."

She calmed herself. She let herself feel that panic and then feel relief and then feel the safety of her friend.

"Let's try again," he said. He took another breath in, while she let hers out and was able to slip all the way through the ropes.

She was free.

She helped Calef get out. His head was still throbbing, along with his mind, as they walked together down the stairs.

The light slowly faded as they descended, until the world around them was completely dark, yet there were still steps under their feet. They felt like they were walking into Hell. As that feeling sank under their skin, they saw a red glow way beneath them.

The end was near.

They continued for several minutes, the warm light getting bigger and brighter until they could make out their destination. It was a massive underground cave. Thick spires hung from the ceiling and, to their surprise, lava flowed in channels far below, giving the walls their fiery hues and their noses the scent of brimstone.

Calef kept walking through the cave, until he noticed that Rebecca was not by his side. He turned around, and saw that she had stopped.

"What's wrong?" he said. "I don't think this is actual Hell."

She was pointing up and ahead. He looked and he saw a large device, the size of a hovercar, embedded in the rock. Then he noticed that were several of the machines planted throughout the cavern, 19 in all.

"What are those?" Calef asked.

"I'm only a scientist," Rebecca said, "but I'm pretty sure those are atomic bombs."

17

"That's not great," Calef said.

"It's not my favorite thing about this trip so far," Rebecca agreed.

He took another look around. Further inside the cave, he saw Will, Joe and Jeff attaching the explosives they brought from the Sea Eagle to one of the atomic bombs embedded in the wall. Abe was off to the side, unable to watch or help. Calef and Rebecca took off in their direction.

"You have to stop!" Calef shouted.

"This is not going to do what you think it's going to do!" Rebecca added.

The group turned and saw the two running. Will shook his head and Jeff headed back towards them.

"Turn around," Jeff said.

Calef and Rebecca made it to them, now out of breath. He spoke past Jeff to Will.

"What's the plan here?" Calef asked. "You think that blowing all of these up is going to bring warmth back to Earth?"

"Something like that," Will said.

"And this was the plan all along?" Rebecca asked. "We saw the rockets you cleaned up at the asteroid site."

"I know you saw," Will said. "I heard you all talking. And I was barely worried for a minute. I realized your revelations are no real threat. Look, your planet is covered with anti-science conspiracy freaks. I figured that even if you two decided to say something, it would be stirred in with the rest of the crazy shit your people spew."

"Are there even any prophesies?" Calef asked.

"Sure there are," Will said. "You've made it this far. I might as well tell you the whole story. As we all know, Jonah Mesh and the Knights were already well-settled on Flora when we learned an asteroid – Velos – was heading towards Earth.

"Jonah did prophesize that. Was it because he spoke to God? We'll never know. But I think at least a little piece of his prophecy was hope on his part. Because as soon as we found out about Velos, Jonah took it as a sign from God that moving humanity to Flora was His plan, and that Jonah was His chosen savior."

"That's unbelievable," Rebecca said.

"Apparently," Will continued. "Because then we found out the asteroid was changing course. Jonah would not be made a liar, so he put together a clandestine team to build and pilot the rockets that would eventually attach to and steer Velos back to Earth.

"Now, you're going to like this part. A small group of Earthers actually found out about the plan. They called themselves the Hot Bloods. They managed to sabotage one of the four rockets, before they died on the asteroid as it collided into the planet."

"Holy shit," Rebecca said, making a realization. "The asteroid wasn't supposed to hit Australia. It was supposed to land right here."

"Bingo," Will said. "We are, for all intents and purposes, a clean-up crew. I honestly don't know what's going to happen when these bombs blow, but Jonah did prophesize the Earth would go cold, and we believe this cave could restart it."

"Did you know, dad?" Calef asked.

Abe turned to him, his eyes filled with hot tears.

"I did not," Abe said. "Will and Joe were the only ones who knew. They told Jeff when he joined our team. They kept me in the dark until now."

"Then do what's right with me," Calef said. "Help me stop them, father."

Abe took a breath.

"I can't do that, son," he said.

Calef took a step back.

"What are you talking about?" Calef asked. "This is wrong."

"No," Abe said. "This is the plan. It must be done. We must save your world."

"This will not save the world, Abe," Rebecca said. "It will destroy it."

"You think that because you don't have faith," Abe said.

A chirp.

"What was that sound, Will?" Calef asked.

"It's too late," he said. "I just set a timer on our bombs for an hour. When the time runs out, our explosives will detonate, and they will set off every other bomb in this cavern. There is no way to turn off the timer or defuse the bombs. This is what God willed and what God wants."

"Oh, He spoke to you, too?" Calef said.

"Of course," Will said. "He speaks through all of us. We are God with flesh on us."

"That makes sense," Calef said. "I was trying to figure out why God was so full of shit."

Calef pulled out his lasergun. Jeff shot him in the leg and he collapsed to the ground.

"Son!" Abe called, his hand outstretched. Rebecca fell to Calef's side to see if he was okay. Calef was screaming, a hole burned above his knee.

"I told my men not to kill you," Will said. "Abe has been a good friend. Loyal. Faithful. I do not want to destroy his children, no matter how wicked some of them may be. I knew we would still need you on this journey, and I knew that you wouldn't leave all your friends behind, so I allowed for her and I locked the rest up so they couldn't interfere. This is over, Calef. Thank you for your service, but this is where we part."

Will, Joe and Jeff walked past them, back towards the entrance of the cave. Abe took one last look at his son, and followed behind.

Zap.

Everyone looked over at Jeff. He looked different. There was now a hole in his forehead that allowed you to see right through him. He collapsed into a pile of nonelectrical meat.

Alva stood fifty meters away, lasergun drawn. He had shot Jeff right in the face. Maya gasped.

"That wasn't exactly what I meant to do," Alva said. "What the fuck do I do now, Calef?"

"Get these three tied up and on a hovermobile back to the Sea Eagle," Calef said, getting to his feet, able to move but with a severe and painful limp. He put his hand on Rebecca for support.

"What makes you think we'll do that?" Will said.

"Alva, you want to shoot in Will's general direction a few times?" Calef asked.

"Fine!" Will said, arms in the air. "You can't stop these bombs."

"I'm not going to stop them," Calef said. "I'm going to move them."

18

Alva and Maya tied up Will and Joe, using the rope previously used on Calef and Rebecca.

"We're going to need Jeff's body for a proper burial," Will said.

"Your plan is to blow our planet the fuck up," Alva said. "Fuck your proper burial."

Alva put Will and Joe in a storage unit in the back of his vehicle; Maya let Abe sit behind her. They all took one last look at the doorway to the underground cave, and then headed back to the Sea Eagle.

Calef and Rebecca were examining the Knight's explosive device and how it was attached. Since it wasn't built to last, they had just used long screws to adhere the bombs in place. They looked through the tools the team had brought down with them and found the drill they needed. Calef started taking out the screws.

"This is wild," he said.

"Just another Tuesday," she said.

"More or less," he said. "So – you and Alva, huh?"

"Me and Alva, finally," she said. "Well, if we make it out of this alive, which feels very unlikely."

"When we get this back on the hovermobile, I'm going to take it as far out as I can," he said. "Alone."

"You are not, Calef," she said. "We do everything together. This is no exception."

"Rebecca," he said. "Someone has to be here. For Joan, at least. Can you imagine how devastated she would be if she lost both of us?"

"Don't say that," she said. Her stomach turned at the thought of a sad dog. "We need to do this together because that's going to be the only way we both survive this. And we have to. We have to live."

"You are stubborn as hell," he said.

"And you have one leg," she said. They both smiled.

"Why can't people believe in things in a healthy way?" he asked.

"I don't know," she said. "It's a distinctly human disease."

"You read or watch old fairy tales?" he asked.

"Sometimes," she said.

"You know Star Wars?" he asked.

"I've heard of it," she said, half-joking, as Calef brought it up frequently. "Fantasy isn't my thing."

"It's science fiction," he said.

"It is not," she said.

"Shut up," he said, laughing. "Oscar has taught us so much about all the different religions, and all the crazy shit people believe in. Some of it makes sense to me. I dig the Tao. I dig Zen. But the thing that makes the most sense to me is the Force."

"The stuff that the guys in the robes use to do telekinesis and control minds?"

"Yes and no, and they're called Jedi, have some respect. Not the supernatural stuff. The idea that the universe itself is a living being. No God. Just the universe, alive, like us, with us. A universe that can think and can feel and listens to us, that created us so we can marvel at it and appreciate it. A universe that can change and can experience expansion and endure entropy. It can be all around us or it can be us. And, sure, there's a dark side, and a light side, but they're not separate; they exist together in the same thing, and what happens depends on how you decide to use it."

"So you believe in a fairy tale?" she asked.

"Among other things," he said. "You know, the Bible and Star Wars are basically the same thing, but one speaks truth without pretending that it's true."

"I wasn't sure if this was Hell before," she said, "but I am sure now. Hell is listening to you talk about pop culture like it means something."

"It does mean something," he said, removing the last screw. They pulled the device from the wall. It was not light. But the Knights knew this, and they had installed wheels on it. They pulled it back towards the stairs, acutely aware that their time was running out.

Every lift up every step was a struggle. But they developed a rhythm, and the way up didn't feel as long as the indeterminate way down. There was no light at the end of the tunnel this time; it had become night while they were down below.

They got the device into the back of the hovermobile it was carried in. There was just about twenty minutes left on the timer.

"Okay," he said, detailing his idea, "we're going to drive east for about fifteen minutes, leave the hovermobile with the bombs wherever we land, and then drive like hell back and hope for the best. That sounds like a solid plan to save the world, no?"

"No," she said. "But it will have to do."

They got on their separate crafts and started driving east. The initial trek was slow as they found their way out of the woods, but then they got on an open patch of uneven ice and started driving as fast as they could.

A crack.

"Did you hear that?" she asked through their comms.

"I did," he said. "Ice cracks. It happens all the time. It's dark so I need you to focus ahead."

He wasn't kidding. Even though their hovermobiles had headlights, their beams were small and focused, and it had continued to snow tremendously. The wind was whipping bitter flakes into their faces, and their vehicles were bobbing up and down on the unforgiving terrain in icy, choppy waves. Their instincts were hard to trust or even touch as they felt remote; they had seemingly stayed behind to hide among the trees.

Another crack.

"It's not normal," she said.

"It's normal," he said.

Another crack.

"It's feeling less normal," he said.

"No shit," she said. "Should we just abandon it here?"

"We can keep going for another few kilometers," he said, and as he said it, he turned his head back to see how far away they had gotten. Rebecca suddenly stopped, disappearing from sight. When he swung his neck back around, the massive snowbank came into view. Calef collided right into it, flying up from his craft into the sharp shards frozen on the hill. His vehicle sputtered before dying completely.

A succession of cracks followed, like a string of fireworks.

"Calef!" she shouted. She moved forward carefully, through pouring snowfall and lukewarm fog. She stopped just shy of the forbidding water.

They had run into a part of Lake Superior that was still a lake in the water sense. Calef's crash had separated a piece of ice from the rest of the land. He was floating alone away from Rebecca. Just him, his hovermobile, and a pile of bombs, drifting upon an iceberg.

It was unsympathetically quiet. There was no one around to care about Calef's fate but nature herself. He continued to drift, further and further away, and Rebecca's voice was already a memory. He was awake; he was full of pain.

That familiar feeling in his fingers and toes started to slip away. He had never felt more alive. He knew that, soon, he would be dead.

He crawled down to his craft. He was relieved the explosive hadn't detonated on impact, but knew that relief was to be short-lived. He found the timer on the device. He had less than three minutes left.

He didn't know how to spend these last few moments. He considered whether he had any regrets. He had very little.

The people he loved knew that he loved them. He had made mistakes, but he learned from them and he changed. He tried to take care of anyone who needed him. He had been cruel. He was kind.

But, most of all, he lived.

He lived in the moment. He spoke his mind. He listened. He knew that he didn't know anything. He recognized that here and now is all we have.

His only regret was that there was no more here, and there was no more now.

He hoped he wouldn't destroy everyone he knew when he was gone.

The final seconds ticked away. He knew if he stayed on the iceberg, there was no doubt that it would be game over, so he pulled his way over to the side of the sheet of frozen land and rolled his way into the frigid waters of Lake Superior.

He was completely submerged and drowning. Brilliant streaks of blue broke through the water's surface to deliver a light show he would have loved to capture with paint. He admired the cool colors as they faded to black, as he sank further and further away from the land and air and the moon.

Death happened like he was told it would happen. He saw a bright light. He figured at this point his brain was releasing chemicals to make his last moments euphoric, but he was still so cold. He tried to reach for the light, but he was still weighed down by so much cold and water. Now the light was getting further away. This was not how he was told death was going to happen.

There was an explosion of bubbles above him. The bombs had gone off, and the force pushed Calef even further down into the abyss. He couldn't tell which way was up, as every direction was decidedly dark to him now.

As soon as Calef stopped reaching for the light, something from the abyss reached out for him.

A giant metal claw wrapped itself around Calef's body. A chain attached to the claw tightened, and it began to pull him up towards the surface. The light was getting exceedingly closer, but as it overtook every part of him, everything became black again, and Calef lost consciousness.

Calef wasn't sure if he was alive or dead. All he knew for certain was that he was somewhere in between.

19

Calef gasped.

A real world breath of air.

He was tingling, but he wasn't dead yet.

Alva and Maya had made it back to the Sea Eagle. Abe told the entire crew what had happened, and how they had been deceived. Most of them were horrified, and all of them felt betrayed on several levels. Will and Joe were put into a safe room, the door locked indefinitely behind them.

Then Abe pleaded for them to save his son.

With the overwhelming blessing of the crew, the Sea Eagle got off the ground and were able to track the hovermobiles that Calef and Rebecca were operating. They arrived just as the explosives were detonated, but they sent an all-terrain smartjaw, outfitted with cameras and heat sensors, through the debris in an effort to save Calef.

The effort wasn't for nothing.

An hour later, Calef was awake and healing nicely in the medical bay. Modern Floran medicine was exceedingly efficient and relatively painless, the absence of pain a nice change of pace for him. There was a mug of steaming coffee on the table to his side. Behind that mug was Maya sitting in a chair.

"Did you have a nice trip?" she asked.

"Shut up," he said, plopping his head back on a pillow. "I'm sorry I forgot to send you a postcard."

"I heard you were busy," she said.

"My vacation was the bomb," he said.

"That should have been the postcard," she said.

"I have to talk to my dad," he said, sitting up in bed.

"You have to rest," she said, standing up to put him back down.

"I will," he said. "I'll be right back."

He groaned as he swung his legs over the sheets. The wound where he was shot was already almost fully healed, but he could still feel it. He pressed his bare toes onto the icy floor and took baby steps into the hallway. He navigated himself to his cabin, and was surprised to see his father sitting on his cot.

The house lights dimmed. He knew it would be the final act of this story.

Act III

ABE: You should not be out and about.

CALEF: We didn't finish our conversation earlier. You said you wished I believed in something like you do. I do. Believe in things, I mean.

ABE: And what is that, my son?

CALEF walks over to the corner of the room. He picks up the painting he brought with him, still wrapped in paper. He hands it to his father.

ABE: What is this?

CALEF: Open it.

ABE unwraps the painting. The audience can't see what's on the canvas.

ABE: It's . . . something. *(He examines it.)* What is it?

CALEF: Look at it. I made that when I was experiencing an extraordinarily deep depression. It was real dark, dad. I couldn't stop drinking, I was barely eating and there were entire days I couldn't get out of bed. But one day I did get out of bed, to make that painting, and it helped me get out of that abyss.

ABE: This is what you believe in?

CALEF: Yeah. I believe in art.

ABE: Art will not bring you to Heaven.

CALEF: Art brings Heaven here. I imagine that painting will be hanging in a room someday. Or it'll be in the back of a storage closet. But wherever it is, someone else who is depressed will come across it. And they won't just look at it, they'll see it. They'll understand it. And they'll feel like someone understands them. And it probably won't cure anything. But it will make them feel better in this place for just a moment. And wherever I am, I will know that I did that.

ABE: That is beautiful.

CALEF: It is. I find my higher power everywhere. It's art. It's pop culture, which helps me make sense of this life. It's this world, with its one season. This one season that reminds us we will never be able to go back to any season before.

ABE looks at the painting again.

ABE: We miss you, Calef.

CALEF: I miss you, too. But Earth is my home.

ABE: Why? Flora is beautiful.

CALEF: Dad, when mom died, I knew that I was going to be living in winter for the rest of my life, no matter where it was I lived. Staying here on Earth has taught me that we don't need seasons to signify change. Life just changes. Always.

ABE: God gave us Flora so we don't have to suffer.

CALEF: Trust me, I understand wanting my pain to have to mean something. But suffering is not a gift or curse from God. From what I've learned, people who rely on God stand by while other people suffer, and people who care about people don't. God stands by.

ABE: I can see there will be no changing your mind.

CALEF: And that's the whole point. That's the difference between us. You want to change me. I don't want to change you at all. Just the way you see me. I love that you believe in something that makes your life better. I think you're perfect just the way you are.

ABE tears up.

ABE: But you seem sad.

CALEF: I know you think that. And sometimes I am. But people seem to bundle joy and hope together, like you can't be happy if you're not full of hope, or you can't be hopeful if you don't feel happy. That's not true. Some days I'm both, but most days I just try to be one or the other.

ABE: I just wish you were closer to your family.

CALEF: We will be in each other's lives more. I told you that understanding is power. I believe that. I think you and I understand each other more now.

ABE: I think we do.

CALEF pulls his father in for a hug.

"I'm sorry to interrupt, Calef," Ada said from the doorway, no bouquet of roses in hand. "Will says he wants to speak to you."

"This should be interesting," Calef said.

. . .

Calef, accompanied by a handful of guards, approached the safe room. Ada unlocked it, and Calef walked inside. Joe stayed seated, his eyes never leaving the floor. He was clearly distraught and knew he wouldn't have the right words to say. Will, on the other hand, knew exactly what he wanted to say.

"No hard feelings, right?" Will asked.

"Is that why you brought me down here?" Calef asked. "Forgiveness?"

"No," Will said, extending his hand. "I'm here to offer you my word."

"All offense meant," Calef said, "but your word means absolutely nothing to me."

"When I get back to Flora, all this," Will said, gesturing to the world around him, "will be resolved. This won't even be a blip. I won't lose a follower. I won't lose one ounce of power."

"What is your offer?" Calef asked.

"I promise not to come back to your planet as long as you are still alive," Will said. He extended his hand further.

"So I'm just supposed to take your word for it? A handshake?" Calef asked.

"That's all humankind has been doing since the beginning of its existence," Will said. Calef looked at him, his disbelief evolving into understanding, and then shook his hand.

Whatever tool works.

"I won't be seeing you," Will said, wiggling his fingers, as Calef walked out of the room.

. . .

He heard her before he saw her.

Joan was barking as loud as she could, bounding down the hallway to leap onto her favorite person. Calef smiled, until Joan ran past Calef and jumped on top of Rebecca, who had been walking hand-in-hand with Alva right behind him.

"Told you!" Rebecca said, taking Joan kisses all over her face.

"Get over here!" Calef commanded, and Joan bounced backwards to him, knocking him on his ass. Joan licked him in all of his unprotected areas. He bathed in her joy.

"We are back in Minneapolis," Ada notified them, sliding her glasses up her nose.

They returned to their cabins to get the rest of their belongings. Calef gave the painting to his father; he gave him and his siblings hugs, and sincere promises that he would see them soon. They expressed gratitude all around. He met up with Rebecca and Alva, who were already waiting on the elevator.

"Where's Joan?" he asked.

Joan was snuggled next to Maya, who didn't look thrilled that Calef was home.

"See you around?" he asked.

"Maybe," she said. "Do you think Earth has room for one more?"

"Maybe," he said. "As long as you're not a fan of beaches or sun tans."

She stood up and walked over to Calef. Unable to stop, she connected her lips to his and they kissed for a moment, each feeling out the other's rhythm, then making one up together of their own.

"I do have to go back to Flora to report everything that's happened here," she said. "But I'll come back."

"That's what they all say," Calef said. He felt slightly embarrassed that he believed she was going to drop everything for him right here and now.

Calef, Joan, Rebecca and Alva waved their final goodbye to the crew, and were lowered down just meters away from Oscar's front door. They trudged their way up and knocked on the door, knowing that it was late, and the old man was probably sleeping.

Instead, he opened the door and invited them in.

"Where's my painting?" he asked.

"Turns out it belonged to someone else," Calef said. They got inside and shut the door.

"I thought it might," Oscar said.

"We have a card game to finish, right?" Rebecca asked.

"You're still not dealing," Oscar said. "The dog can deal before I let you."

There was a knock at the door.

"I think that's for you, big guy," Alva said, lightly punching Calef on the shoulder. He went back to the front door and opened it. It was Maya.

"You never answered my question," she said. "What was the first thing you thought when you saw me?"

"I wanted to tell you how beautiful I thought you were," he said.

"Ugh. I do not care for subjective opinions about external beauty. Do you have space at your card table for one more?" she asked.

"Thought you had things to do," he said.

"I'm here, now," she said. "And since meeting you, all I want to be is here, now, with you. Is that okay?"

"That's okay," he said, and he kissed her again, getting familiar with their rhythm.

They gathered around the table, a family of strangers who found and chose each other in this cold world, and they played another hand.

The End

Words & Worlds by Dennis Vogen

Made in the USA
Middletown, DE
30 April 2022

64924074R00129